HOOKY

VOLUME 2

MÍRIAM BONASTRE TUR

CLARION BOOKS
IMPRINTS OF HARPERCOLLINSPUBLISHERS

CLARION BOOKS IS AN IMPRINT OF HARPERCOLLINS PUBLISHERS.
HARPERALLEY IS AN IMPRINT OF HARPERCOLLINS PUBLISHERS.

ISBN 978-0-35-869309-3 PAPERBACK
ISBN 978-0-35-869310-9 HARDCOVER
ISBN 978-0-06-327362-7 SIGNED EDITION

LETTERING BY NATALIE FONDRIEST

22 23 24 25 26 RTLO 10 9 8 7 6 5 4 3 2 1

FIRST EDITION
A DIGITAL VERSION OF *HOOKY* WAS ORIGINALLY PUBLISHED ON WEBTOON IN 2015.

CHAPTER 33
NICO, YOU'RE GOING TOO FAR.
SOMETHING SIMILAR HAPPENED TO DORIAN ON THE FLOATING ROCK.
HE LOST CONTROL OF HIMSELF.
YES, BUT HE LOST IT BECAUSE OF THE URGE TO PROTECT DANI.
BUT DANI...
SHE WAS SEEKING REVENGE.
I DON'T THINK ANYONE'S FOLLOWING US...
BUT WHERE CAN WE GO?
WE'RE HOMELESS.
WE CAN'T GO BACK TO THE CASTLE!
CALM DOWN! WE'LL FIGURE IT OUT.
YOU CAN STAY AT MASTER'S HOUSE.

MASTER PENDRAGON WAS AT THE PALACE...
MAYBE HE WAS CAPTURED.
MAYBE. BUT HE'LL FIND A WAY OUT AND COME LOOKING FOR US. I TRUST HIM.
IT CAN'T BE...
WHAT?!

MASTER'S HOUSE...

THEY DID THIS! WE'LL DESTROY THEM.
MARK, THEY'RE WITCHES. THEY SAY HILDE WYTTE SENT THEM.
IT'S BEST IF WE LAY LOW FOR NOW.

BUT, DAD—
HE'S RIGHT.

BUT, NICO, YOUR HOUSE—!
WE'RE NOT PREPARED TO FIGHT.

ANYWAY, MASTER ALWAYS TOLD US TO PLAY IT SAFE.
MAYBE WE SHOULD PAY ATTENTION, FOR ONCE.

YOU HEARD NICO, MARK. TAKE THEM AWAY FROM HERE.
I KNOW THE PERFECT PLACE.

NICO, WHERE ARE YOU GOING?
HURRY UP!
IS EVERYBODY HERE?
THERE'S A CABIN IN THE WOODS. IT'S WHERE MY FRIENDS USED TO HANG OUT ON WEEKENDS.
DANI... CAREFUL.
WE MADE IT.
NOW WHAT?

I CAN'T DO MAGIC. I CAN'T FIGHT.
I'M MORE USELESS THAN EVER.
AND WE'RE ON OUR OWN.

THREE MONTHS LATER
DANI!
AH! HI, DORIAN.
SOMEONE'S GOING TO SEE YOU! WHAT ARE YOU DOING?

DO I REALLY NEED TO WEAR THIS HORRIBLE HAT? IT'S ALL SCRUFFY!

IF WE RUN INTO A WITCH, WE WANT TO BE IN DISGUISE.

...IF YOU'RE LOOKING FOR MONICA, SHE'S NOT HERE.

WHAT ARE YOU TALKING ABOUT?!

I WASN'T LOOKING FOR HER. I CAME IN FOR WATER.
YEAH, SURE.

AND WHERE... WHERE DID SHE SAY SHE—
SHE WENT DOWN THE PLANK PATH.

HA-HA, HE DIDN'T LAST LONG!

COME ON...

I CAN DO IT...
COME ON...

MOVE.
MOVE...

ONE...

TWO...

MOVE!!

DARN IT.

TRY TO FOCUS ON THE SURROUNDINGS.
!

WHAT ARE YOU DOING HERE?
I WANTED TO DO IT BY MYSELF!
I'M SORRY! I JUST WANTED TO HELP.

I DON'T NEED YOUR HELP. YOU'VE TAUGHT ME ENOUGH.
SIT DOWN AND OBSERVE.
AS YOU WISH, YOUR HIGHNESS.

THE SURROUNDINGS...?
YES, I REMEMBER READING SOMETHING ABOUT THAT.
I MUST FOCUS THE SPELL NOT ONLY ON THE OBJECT IN QUESTION...

BUT ON EVERYTHING THAT TOUCHES IT.

IN THAT CASE...
THE WATER?
YES!
WHA—

LOOK, DORIAN!
I DID IT! BY MYSELF! I'M INCREDIBLE!
WELL...I ACTUALLY THINK IT WAS THANKS TO ME—
WHAT DID YOU JUST SAY?!
UH...NEVER MIND, IT WAS ONLY A LITTLE INPUT AFTER ALL.
VERY LITTLE!
AT LEAST 20%
...WELL, ALL RIGHT, THEN.
WE'RE REALLY CLOSE.

EVEN AFTER THREE MONTHS...
IT'S STILL DEPRESSING.
I'M OKAY.
NICO...?
THERE'S A LOT OF GARBAGE...
I WONDER IF THERE'S ANYTHING WORTH SALVAGING.
WHAT—
MASTER'S CRYSTAL BALL?!

IT'S PRINCE WILLIAM!
DID YOU FIND SOMETHING?
YEAH! SOMETHING AWESOME.
HURRY UP, WE NEED TO SHOW EVERYONE!
WHAT IS IT?
I KNOW WHERE PRINCE WILLIAM IS.
AND WE'RE GONNA FIND HIM!

CAN ANYONE PASS ME SOME BLACK PEPPER?
HOW MANY CHAIRS DO WE NEED?
WILL NICO AND MARK BE HOME FOR DINNER?
YES, THE VILLAGE IS CLOSE.
THEY SHOULD BE BACK ANY TIME NOW.
DORIAN'S BEING LAZY AS ALWAYS...
CAN'T YOU HELP?
THE BLACK PEPPER IS ON THE HIGHER SHELF.
AND YOU AREN'T DOING MUCH EITHER, IVY!
WE'RE DOING THE PRINCESS'S HAIR! ARE YOU SUGGESTING MONICA'S HAIR IS NOT IMPORTANT?
I FOUND IT! AND I HAVEN'T DROPPED ANY OF—
ARGH!
HEY, EVERYONE! I'VE GOT SOME GOOD NEWS!
WE FOUND SOMETHING.
ND EVEN MORE IMPORTANT...
I KNOW WHERE PRINCE WILLIAM IS!
HUH?
WHAT? ARE YOU SERIOUS?!

THIS IS THE MASTER'S CRYSTAL BALL.
IT'S SO SHINY...
I CAN'T SEE ANYTHING.
HANG ON A SECOND...

SEE? THERE HE IS!
THAT'S HIM, RIGHT, PRINCESS?

IT LOOKS LIKE HE'S IN A CAVE... OR A TOWER...
AND THERE'S THE DRAGON! WE FOUND HIM!
UH... NICO...

I CAN'T SEE ANYTHING.

NEITHER CAN I.
HUH?
I CAN'T EITHER...
WHAT?
IT'S JUST A SHINY BALL...

B-BUT... IT'S RIGHT HERE!
IT'S A MESSAGE FROM THE MASTER. I'M SURE OF IT!

HE'S ONLY DOING IT TO LOOK IMPORTANT. HE MUST THINK WE'RE FOOLS.
NO, I'M REALLY SEEING IT!
I CAN ALSO SEE CITIES WITH HUGE WALLS FULL OF ARCHES AND TOWERS...

THAT SOUNDS JUST LIKE HOME, TO BE HONEST.
I DON'T TRUST YOU EITHER, AMIR.

DON'T BE SO MEAN, IVY!
I BELIEVE YOU, NICO.

REALLY?
YOU KNOW WHAT I THINK?

I THINK YOU HAVE THE GIFT OF CLAIRVOYANCE, JUST LIKE THE MASTER.
IT'S A VERY RARE TYPE OF MAGIC THAT'S ALMOST IMPOSSIBLE TO LEARN.

THAT'S WHY IT'S SO COOL THAT YOU CAN DO IT! HOW LUCKY!
THAT DOESN'T MAKE ANY SENSE...
I COULD NEVER DO MAGIC...

I WAS ALWAYS ABLE TO SEE WHAT WAS IN THE MASTER'S BALL...

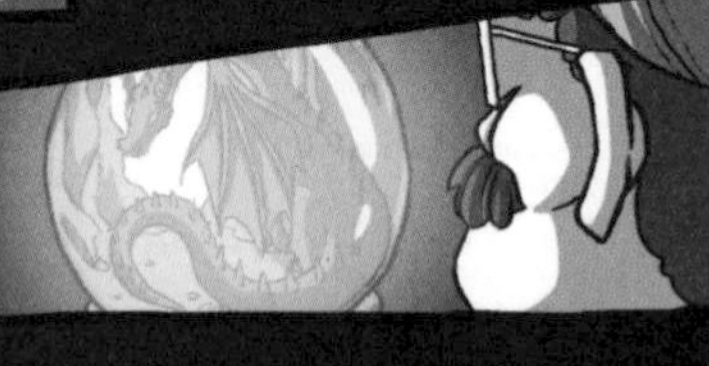

BUT I THOUGHT THAT WAS NORMAL.
HE NEVER TOLD ME THE TRUTH. HE NEVER TOLD ME...
THAT I WAS A WITCH.

I'M CLAIRVOYANT?!

THAT'S AMAZING, NICO! NOW WE'LL BE ABLE TO FIND MY DEAR WILL. WE NEED TO LEAVE AS SOON AS POSSIBLE!

I DIDN'T EVEN THINK TELLING THE FUTURE WAS POSSIBLE BEFORE I MET THE MASTER. YOU'LL NEED TO SHOW ME HOW TO DO IT!

WHOA...YOU REALLY *ARE* A WITCH!

CONGRATULATIONS, NICO! YOU REALLY ARE THE MASTER'S APPRENTICE.
CAN YOU TELL OUR FUTURES?

IT SEEMS LIKE EVERYONE HERE CAN DO MAGIC!
WHAT ELSE DID YOU SEE IN THE CRYSTAL BALL?
HOW DID WILLIAM LOOK, REALLY?

EVERYBODY, SHUT UP!
THERE HE GOES...

SHOULD WE INTERVENE?
NO... HE'LL BE FINE.
HE'S UNDERSTANDABLY OVERWHELMED.

HIS ENTIRE LIFE JUST CHANGED.

...
NICO AND MARK BROUGHT THAT FROM THE MASTER'S HOUSE, RIGHT?
WILL YOU WEAR IT AGAIN?

NO.

I'LL STICK TO BLACK. WITCHES AREN'T THE ISSUE, AFTER ALL.
THE ISSUE...?

YOU KNOW WHAT I MEAN, DORIAN...
I'VE THOUGHT ABOUT IT LONG AND HARD...
ARE WITCHES EVIL? OR ARE THE PEOPLE WHO FEAR WITCHES TO BLAME?
SHOULD I EMBRACE MY MAGIC, DESPITE NOT BEING ABLE TO CONTROL IT?
AND WHAT ABOUT THE PROPHECIES...?

WE CAN'T RUN AWAY FROM OUR DESTINY... IT'S ALREADY BEEN WRITTEN.

BUT WHAT IF WE COULD?
WHAT IF WE COULD CHANGE THINGS? *FIX* THINGS?

DOING THE RIGHT THING... TOGETHER... CAN WE CHANGE THE FUTURE?
I BELIEVE SO.
YOU DO?
MHM.

WE NEED TO GET STARTED RIGHT AWAY!
FIRST, WE'LL FIND THE PRINCE. THEN WE'LL SAVE EVERYBODY ELSE! THE MASTER, THE KING, DAD, MOM, DAMIEN...
EVERYONE! RIGHT?

LET'S TALK ABOUT OUR MAGIC CLASSES THEN.
CLASSES?!
YOU HAVEN'T STUDIED FOR THREE MONTHS, DANI!
YOU NEED TO BECOME STRONGER!
ARE YOU TRYING TO BRIBE ME TO STUDY WITH COOKIES?
SEE, NICO? DANI'S STILL THE SAME AS ALWAYS.

YOU MIGHT BE RIGHT.
I CAUGHT THE THIEF, EVERYBODY! DORIAN TOOK THE COOKIES.
DID YOU THINK WE WOULDN'T FIND YOU?
ARGH! YOU'RE SUCH TATTLERS.
TOO LATE! WE ALREADY ATE THEM ALL!

CHAPTER 34
THREE...
FOUR...
FIVE...
SIX...
UH... SEVEN...
EIGHT...
NINE...
AND TEN!
READY OR NOT, HERE I COME!
I FOUND YOU!
NOOO!
HE-HE...
YOU'RE ALL SO BAD AT HIDING.
I'M GONNA WIN!
AHA!
I FOUND DA—
WHOAAAA!
IS THAT LIGHTNING?!
ARE YOU TWO OKAY?

RIBBIT?
WHAT HAPPENED...?
DAMIEN...

I DIDN'T... SNIFF...DO IT ON PURPOSE...
THAT'S ALL RIGHT, SWEETHEART.
THEY GOT A LITTLE SCARED, THAT'S NORMAL.
BUT I'M SURE YOU'LL MAKE UP SOON.
REALLY...?
OF COURSE. JUST WAIT AND SEE.
DON'T LIE TO THE CHILD. THIS IS THE WORST THING THAT COULD HAVE HAPPENED TO US.
DON'T BE SO EXTREME, HONEY.
DAMIEN DIDN'T DO IT ON PURPOSE. AND THE CHILD IS ALREADY BACK TO NORMAL.
NOW THE WHOLE VILLAGE KNOWS WE'RE WITCHES.
WE'LL BE OUTCASTS!

AGH!
WAHH!
YOU MADE HIM CRY AGAIN!
AM I IN TROUBLE?

NO, DAMIEN.
IT'S JUST UNTIL THINGS CALM DOWN.

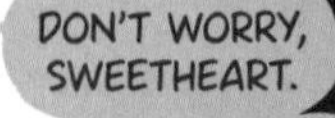

WE NEED TO KEEP SAFE.
PEOPLE CAN BE DANGEROUS WHEN THEY'RE SCARED.
HANS, COME ON... IT'S NOT LIKE THEY BURN WITCHES ANYMORE!

OH NO!
HAVE THEY LOST THEIR MINDS?
THEY HAVE WEAPONS...
HURRY UP, WE NEED TO GET AWAY FROM THE WINDOW.
LET'S GET OUT OF HERE.
THE BROOMS ARE IN THE SHED!
TAKE THE CHILD, HANS!
CAN YOU RUN, HON—?
FREEZE, WITCH!

SHE'S THREATENING US!
SHE'S A WITCH.
MUM...!
SHE'S EVIL!

MAYBE YOUR KING HAS FORBIDDEN IT... BUT I DON'T AGREE.

ALL WITCHES SHOULD BURN. IT'S YOUR FATE.

BURN THE WITCH!
SHE'S A MONSTER!

COME HERE, SON.
I'M SORRY, DAMIEN.
I'M SO SORRY.

DAD... MUM IS...
WE'LL MAKE THEM PAY FOR THIS.

NO MATTER WHAT.
THEY'LL PAY.
I PROMISE...

...ANGELA.
AAAARGH!
STOP!
WHAT IS ALL THIS?
KING GEORGE!?
THE KING IS HERE!

MOM SURVIVED AND I FELT SO DEEPLY RELIEVED.

BUT SOMETHING WASN'T QUITE RIGHT.

A STRANGE AURA SURROUNDED HER, DARK AND MAGICAL.
SAY SOMETHING, MY LOVE.
IF YOU WON'T TALK TO ME, I...
I DON'T KNOW WHAT I'LL DO...

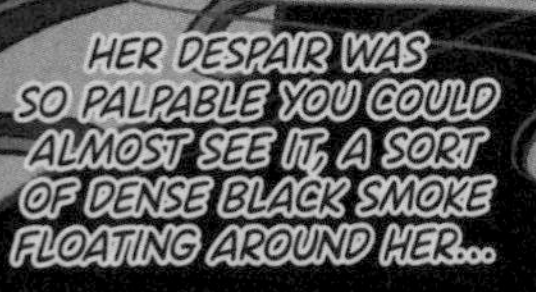
HER DESPAIR WAS SO PALPABLE YOU COULD ALMOST SEE IT, A SORT OF DENSE BLACK SMOKE FLOATING AROUND HER...

CASTING A SHADOW ON EVERYTHING.
THE FEELING THAT HAD BEEN BUILDING UP AT THE BOTTOM OF MY STOMACH STARTED TAKING SHAPE,

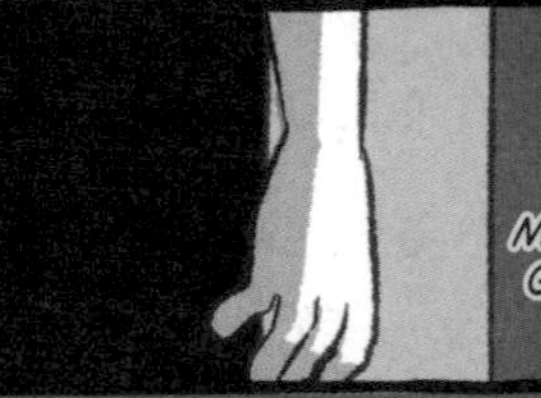
SMOTHERING ME LITTLE BY LITTLE, GETTING STRONGER, MORE REAL.

IT BECAME A THOUGHT AND THEN A CERTAINTY.

IT WAS ALL MY FAULT.

I HAD SHOWN MY MAGIC TO PEOPLE AND BECAUSE OF THAT, WE HAD ALL BEEN HUNTED.

MY MOM WAS HURTING BECAUSE OF ME.

MOM IS ALL RIGHT, DON'T WORRY.
LOOK. MEET YOUR SISTER AND YOUR BROTHER.

WOW!!

CAN I HOLD THEM, DAD?
BE CAREFUL...

WE HAVE TO NAME THE BABIES... ANGELA?
...

...
HANS...

...!
TELL ME.
I CAN'T GO ON LIKE THIS.
I'M WASTING AWAY.

EVEN IF MY MOTHER WAS SMILING AGAIN, HER SMILE WAS COLD AND ODD.

I JUST WANTED MY MOM TO BE THE SAME PERSON THAT SHE WAS BEFORE.

DID YOU SHOW MERCY WHEN YOU CONDEMNED MY FAMILY?
BUT WE'VE ALREADY LEFT YOU ALONE!
WHAT ELSE DO YOU WANT?
DON'T YOU SEE WHAT YOU'VE DONE TO HER?!
WHAT CAN WE DO ABOUT THAT?
I...I WANT JUSTICE! YOU DESTROYED MY FAMILY.
A ROTTEN FAMILY! KILLING WITCHES IS JUSTICE.
WHAT...?!
HOW DARE YOU?!
DAD...?
WHAT HAVE YOU DONE??

IT GOT OUT OF HAND...
I—
THOSE ARE MY FRIEND'S PARENTS!
YOU...
YOU *ARE* A MONSTER! I HATE YOU!

DON'T RAISE YOUR VOICE AT YOUR FATHER. IT'S MY DUTY TO PROTECT THIS FAMILY!
TO MAKE THE WORLD RESPECT WITCHES.
YOU SAW WHAT HAPPENS WHEN PEOPLE DISRESPECT US. SOMEONE GETS HURT.

YOUR MOTHER'S RIGHT.
WE CAN'T PRETEND NOTHING HAS HAPPENED.
DAMIEN, YOU'RE THE WYTTE FAMILY HEIR. ONE DAY, IT WILL BE YOUR DUTY TO MAKE SURE WE ARE RESPECTED.

IF THAT'S TRUE...I DON'T WANT TO BE THE HEIR OF THIS FAMILY!

I WAS CONFUSED.

HORRIFIED. SCARED.

ALONE.

I WAS SMOTHERED WITH GUILT.

AND WITH HATE.

MOM...

I'M SO GLAD WE'RE LIVING TOGETHER AGAIN, LIKE A FAMILY...
I HOPE WE FIND YOUR SIBLINGS SOON.

WHERE IS PRINCE WILLIAM?

BUT YOU NEED TO GET SERIOUS ABOUT YOUR DUTIES AS KING...

WHERE'S WILLIAM, MOM?

YOUR FATHER AND AUNT BOTH THINK THEY ARE IN A POSITION TO GIVE ORDERS...

MOM!!

I...I WANT TO SEEK REVENGE, AS YOU ASKED.
I WILL KILL THE SON OF THE MAN WHO HURT YOU.
I'LL KILL WILLIAM.
BUT IN ORDER TO DO THAT, I NEED TO KNOW WHERE HE IS.

I'M SORRY, MOM.

WE'LL GET HIS FATHER AND MONICA RIGHT WHERE WE WANT THEM.

REVENGE WON'T HEAL YOU.

CHAPTER 35

ARE YOU SURE YOU WANT TO STAY, NOAH?

YEAH...SOMEONE HAS TO LOOK AFTER THIS PLACE.
PLUS, WE CAN'T LEAVE ALEX ALONE.
AND WE HAVE NOWHERE TO GO.
WELL...

WE WON'T LET YOU DOWN.
WE'LL FIND PRINCE WILLIAM. AND THEN WE'LL MAKE EVERYBODY SEE SENSE!
PEACE WILL PREVAIL AND JUSTICE WILL BE DONE!
ALEX WOULD BE SO PROUD...
I CAN HEAR HER THROUGH YOUR VOICE.

...NOAH
THANK YOU SO MUCH!

I'M SO GLAD WE MET. I HOPE WE'LL SEE EACH OTHER SOON!
YOU'RE AMAZING. YOU ALL ARE!
AWW, LOOK AT THEM, CRYING TOGETHER.
HOW SOULFUL.

YOU TOO?!
IT'S JUST SO...SNIFF...SO BEAUTIFUL...
GUH...

HERE, YOU'LL LOOK GREAT IN THIS.
WHAT ARE YOU DOING?
YOU SHOULD WEAR SOMETHING TO HIDE YOUR FACES.

WE DON'T KNOW WHO MIGHT BE WATCHING.
WE'LL LOOK LIKE SPIES!

ALL THIS BLACK IS SO DEPRESSING... COULD YOU CHANGE THE COLOR OF MY HOOD, DORIAN?
BUT, PRINCESS... BLACK IS MANDATORY FOR WITCHES.

IT'S FINE, CUPCAKE BOY. AS LONG AS NOBODY FINDS OUT I'M THE PRINCESS.

THINGS ARE FINALLY STARTING TO LOOK UP.

TODAY IS SUCH A GOOD DAY!

DORIAN.
THERE'S SOMETHING I NEED TO ASK YOU.

SURE. WHAT IS IT?
IT'S ABOUT THE POTION.

WE DIDN'T USE IT ON ALEX WHEN SHE, UH...WHEN SHE GOT HURT.

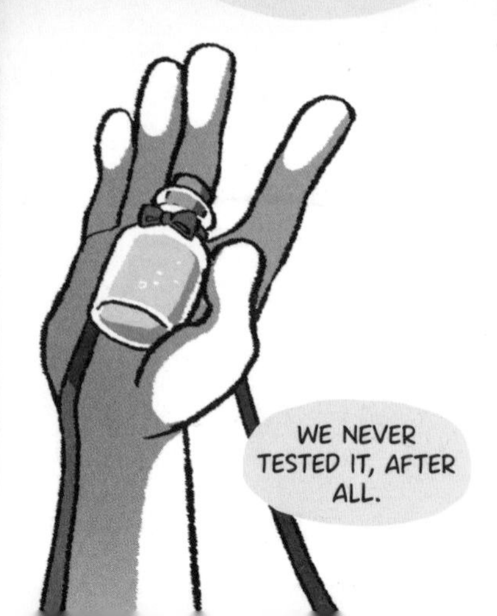
WHY, THOUGH?
DID YOU NOT WANT TO HURT MY FEELINGS BY TELLING ME THAT THE POTION DOESN'T REALLY WORK?
WE NEVER TESTED IT, AFTER ALL.

AM I RIGHT, DORIAN?
OF COURSE NOT!
THE COLOR, THE SMELL, EVERYTHING IN YOUR POTION SEEMS PERFECT. LOOK, I ALWAYS CARRY IT WITH ME IN CASE I NEED IT.

OH, YOU STILL KEEP IT!
OF COURSE, IT'S YOUR FIRST POTION.
BUT...NO POTION CAN BRING SOMEONE BACK TO LIFE.

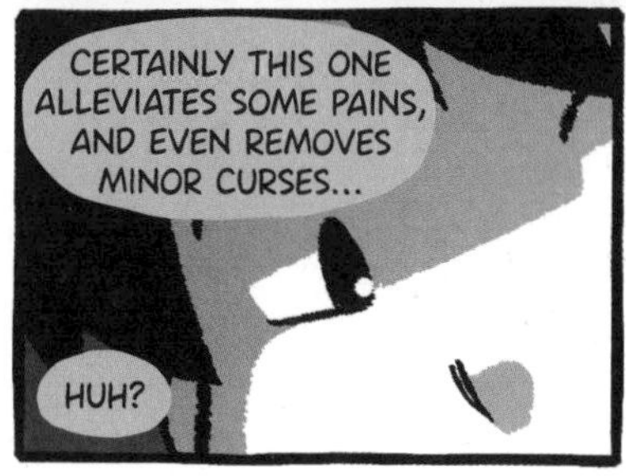
CERTAINLY THIS ONE ALLEVIATES SOME PAINS, AND EVEN REMOVES MINOR CURSES...
HUH?

WHAT'S THAT OTHER NECKLACE YOU'RE WEARING, MONICA?
THIS?

IT'S MY ENGAGEMENT RING.

IS IT WILLIAM'S?
OF COURSE IT IS! HE'S MY FIANCÉ, AFTER ALL.
KNOWING WILLIAM, HE'S PROBABLY ALREADY LOST HIS.
DON'T SAY THAT, AMIR!

YOU KNOW HIM AS WELL AS I DO, MONICA. IT WOULDN'T SURPRISE ME.
WELL... MAYBE...
BUT...

WHY DO YOU WORRY ABOUT IT THAT MUCH?
HUH? WHAT DO YOU MEA—?
HEY, YOU, IN THE TRUCK! PULL OVER, NOW!
WHO IS IT...?
THIS IS A ROUTINE CHECK.
THEY'RE WITCHES!
WE WON'T ALLOW OPPOSERS OF THE KING TO TRAVEL FREELY THROUGHOUT THE KINGDOM.

NOW WHAT?! HOODS WON'T CUT IT!
THE OTHERS ARE ALREADY LEAVING THE TRUCK.

DANI!

CALM DOWN, WE'RE WITCHES!
LOOK, WE HAVE A BLACK CAT AND A CRYSTAL BALL AND EVERYTHING.
ALL RIGHT, KIDS, GO AHEAD.
DON'T FORGET TO WARN THE KING'S MEN IF YOU SEE SUSPICIOUS INDIVIDUALS.
WHAT A PAIN!
THANKS, PALS.
OH, DANI LOOKS LOVELY!

LOVELY?!
THERE'S NO WAY THEY'LL BUY IT.

WHAT?!
WELL, IT WORKED...

NEXT! HURRY UP, WE DON'T HAVE ALL DAY.
THEY'RE COMING!
HURRY UP, DORIAN, YOUR MUSTACHE!
...
MONICA, THEY'LL RECOGNIZE YOU FOR SURE.
THERE MUST BE A SPELL WE CAN USE!
COME ON, COME ON...

I CAN'T THINK OF ANYTHING!
OPEN THE DOOR!

THEY'RE GONNA SMASH THE VAN...!
SHOULD I START THE ENGINE?

YES, ANNE! START IT!
BUT, MONICA, THEY'LL FOLLOW US.

I THINK I HAVE A PLAN.
BUT YOU NEED TO HELP ME!
...OF COURSE.

I SAID OPEN UP!
...HUH?

WHAT ARE THEY DOING?!
THAT WAS DEFINITELY DORIAN'S IDEA.
WE NEED TO DO SOMETHING!

THEY ESCAPED...
LOOKS LIKE THEY'RE WITCHES, AFTER ALL.
CORRECT!
YEAH, BUT THEY RAN FOR A REASON.

NO WAY! THEY'RE ACQUAINTANCES OF OURS.
MAYBE THEY GOT SCARED BECAUSE THEY THOUGHT YOU WERE TRAITORS OR SOMETHING.

GET OUT OF THE WAY.
OUCH!

HEY, THOSE ARE OUR BROOMS!
WE'RE COMMANDEERING THEM, IN KING DAMIEN'S NAME.
SUSPECTS ARE MOVING AWAY AT HIGH SPEED!

MONICA, WHAT SHOULD I DO?!

JUST DRIVE! WE'LL TAKE CARE OF THE REST!

WHOA!
THEY'RE COMING! WITCHES ARE ATTACKING US!

SHE'S RIGHT!
DO SOMETHING!
DORIAN!
IF I BREAK THE SPELL NOW THE TRUCK WILL PLUMMET!
YOU'LL SEE...
ARGH!

WHAT WAS THAT?
AARGH!

OH!
AARGH!

IT'S DANI.

NO ONE IS FOLLOWING US ANYMORE!
LET'S LAND, THEN.
!!
WATCH OUT!!
MONICA!

JACKPOT!
NONE OTHER THAN THE PRINCESS HERSELF!
LET ME GO AT ONCE!
MONICA, GIVE ME YOUR HAND!
LET HER GO!
I CAN'T HIT MONICA BY ACCIDENT...

ARE YOU SURE OF THIS, DANI?
DORIAN WILL CATCH HER!
...I HOPE.

MONICA!
BE CAREFUL!
STAY STILL!
TAKE MY HAND!

I SAID LET ME GO!

OOF.

MONICA!

UM... DORIAN...
THE...
THE SPELL...

WE'RE GONNA FAAAAAAAAAALL!

IT CAN'T BE...
DON'T WORRY, EVERYTHING WILL BE ALL RIGHT...
DANI—

GET OUT OF MY WAY!
I'M COMING WITH YOU.
ARGH!

DORIAN!
MONICA!
AMIR!
ANNE!
THEY MUST BE AROUND HERE...

IT'S A GOOD SIGN THAT THEY'RE NOT HERE.

WHAT DO YOU MEAN?

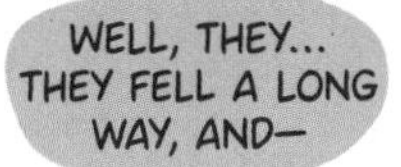
WELL, THEY... THEY FELL A LONG WAY, AND—

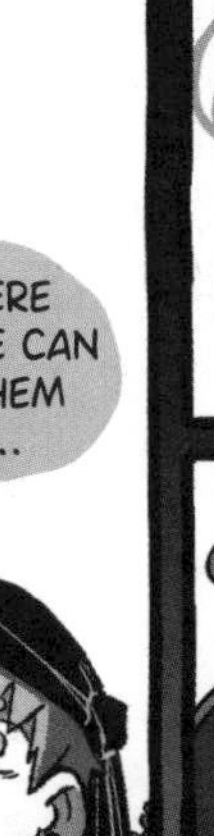
NICO...
IF THEY WERE CAPTURED, WE CAN JUST GET THEM OUT, AND...

WELL, NEVER MIND.

AND IF THEY'RE HERE SOMEWHERE?

WE *ARE* HERE.

DORIAN...!
BUT WE...

WE LOST MONICA.

DID SHE FALL?
I... I HOPE NOT.
THAT GUY HAD A BROOM. HOPEFULLY SHE WAS ABLE TO USE IT TO FLY.

HEY, PSYCHIC GUY! LOOK IN THAT DAMN CRYSTAL BALL AND TELL US IF MONICA'S ALIVE.
I'M TRYING!

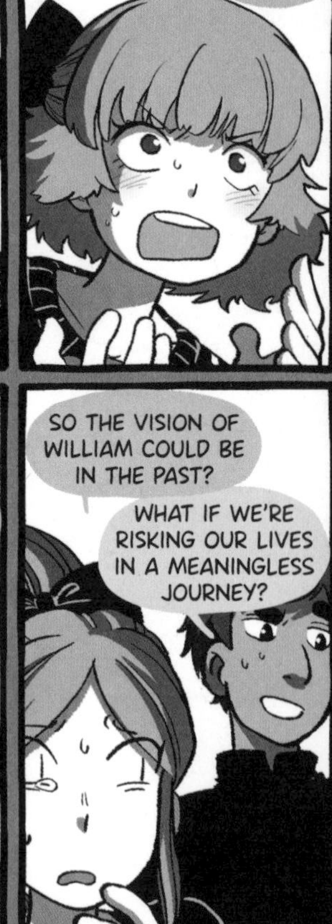
BUT I DON'T KNOW HOW THIS WORKS.
I DON'T EVEN KNOW IF I'M LOOKING TO THE PAST OR THE PRESENT.
FREAKING USELESS!
LEAVE HIM ALONE, IVY.
I DON'T NEED YOU TO SPEAK FOR ME.
SO THE VISION OF WILLIAM COULD BE IN THE PAST?
WHAT IF WE'RE RISKING OUR LIVES IN A MEANINGLESS JOURNEY?

AND MAYBE IT'S TOO LATE FOR MONICA—
ENOUGH!

FIGHTING ISN'T GOING TO SOLVE ANYTHING.
WE NEED TO START LOOKING FOR HER RIGHT NOW.

SHE CAN'T BE THAT FAR—
HEY, BRATS!

WHAT HAVE YOU DONE TO US?!

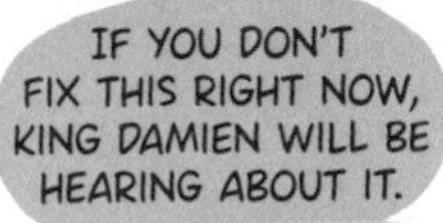

IF YOU DON'T FIX THIS RIGHT NOW, KING DAMIEN WILL BE HEARING ABOUT IT.
OKAY, THEN... LET'S MAKE A DEAL.
I'LL TELL YOU HOW TO GET BACK TO NORMAL IF YOU TELL ME WHERE YOU TAKE PRISONERS.
...FINE.
WE WERE GOING TO TAKE THEM TO A MAN WHO KEEPS AN EYE ON THE WOODS FOR HILDE WYTTE.
HE LIVES CLOSE BY, BUT THE ROAD'S TOO NARROW TO DRIVE. YOU'LL NEED TO WALK.

OKAY. LET'S GO.
WAIT, I'M COMING!
HEY, KID! WHAT ABOUT OUR DEAL?!

OH, RIGHT!
I ACCIDENTALLY CURSED YOU. I'M ALMOST SURE YOU'LL GO BACK TO NORMAL IF YOU SINCERELY APOLOGIZE.
BYE!

WE'RE HERE...

NOT WHAT I WAS EXPECTING.
HOW SHABBY.
I THINK IT'S KINDA CUTE!

IT'S LOCKED.
MOVE. I'LL KICK IT DOWN.
STOP SHOWING OFF, MAN.

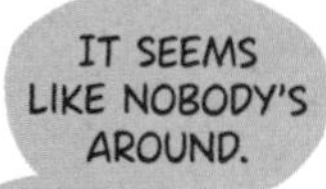

IT SEEMS LIKE NOBODY'S AROUND.
LET'S GO!
HAVE YOU LOST YOUR MINDS?
SOMEONE COULD BE HIDDEN!

EXCUSE ME...

HI, KIDS. HOW CAN I HELP YOU?

FUNNY YOU SHOULD ASK.
BECAUSE WE ARE NOT LEAVING UNTIL YOU TELL US WHAT YOU'VE DONE WITH THE PRINCESS.
HUH?

DORIAN, WAIT...
HE...HE DOESN'T LOOK EVIL.
WE SHOULDN'T BE THREATENING SOMEONE WHO'S PEACEFUL.
YOU HEARD THOSE WITCHES. THIS GUY DETAINS PEOPLE. HE'S OUR ENEMY.

I'M NOT YOUR ENEMY!
I'M NOT A WITCH, AS YOU CAN SEE.

BUT I THINK THE WITCHES' SIDE IS THE RIGHT SIDE.
...THE RIGHT SIDE?
I DON'T THINK THERE IS SUCH A THING.

YOU SEEM NICE...
BUT TURNING THE KING INTO A TOAD AND PERSECUTING THOSE WHO OPPOSE HIS USURPER...
THAT DOESN'T FEEL "RIGHT" AT ALL.

WHERE IS SHE?
YOU BURNED MY HOUSE DOWN.

HE WON'T LAST MUCH LONGER.

GUYS, WAIT—
LAST CHANCE...

DORIAN SEEMS TO HAVE CHOSEN A SIDE.

HE'S QUITE SURE OF IT.

BUT WHAT IF I DON'T WANT TO CHOOSE?

DORIAN SEEMS TO FORGET THAT WE'RE WITCHES, TOO.

WE HAVE SUFFERED...

MORE THAN ANYONE.

WHY DID HE PICK THEIR SIDE, THEN?
IS IT BECAUSE...?
WHY DO I FEEL SO LONELY?

DORIAN, STOP IT.
GIVE HIM A CHANCE TO EXPLAIN.

HE'S ALREADY SAID ENOUGH. DIDN'T YOU HEAR? ALL HE DOES IS DEFEND WITCHES!

THEY'RE NOT NEARLY AS BAD AS YOU THINK—
SHUT YOUR MOUTH OR I'LL SET YOUR SHACK ON FIRE.

STOP!
AH!
DANI! GIVE ME MY WAND!
NO!
NOT UNTIL WE SPEAK LIKE CIVILIZED PEOPLE.
WE DON'T HAVE TIME FOR THIS. GIVE IT BACK!
NO WAY!
AARGH!
OUCH!
COME ON, GUYS... CALM DOWN.
HOW STUPID!

COME ON NOW, THAT'S ENOUGH ARGUING!
UGH.
HEY...!

DANI, STOP FIDGETING.
GIVE ME THE WAND, DORIAN!
NO!

I HONESTLY DIDN'T MEAN TO CAUSE ALL THIS...

WASN'T OUR GOAL TO MAKE EVERYONE GET ALONG?!
UGH...

MONICA MIGHT BE IN DANGER!

THAT'S NOT AN EXCUSE TO HARM INNOCENT PEOPLE!

INNOCENT PEOPLE?!

WITCHES HUNTING OPPOSERS—
ALEX WASN'T KILLED BY WITCHES!!

...
THAT DOESN'T HAVE ANYTHING TO DO WITH THIS.
IT DOESN'T?
WHAT DOES IT HAVE TO DO WITH, THEN?
YOU DON'T CARE...
YOU ONLY CARE ABOUT...
...

YOU'RE SO SELFISH.
I'M SELFISH? THAT'S NOT TRUE!

LET ME GO!
DANI!
DANI, WAIT—

DANI!
WHERE ARE YOU GOING?
OOF, HOW CAN YOU ALL RUN SO FAST?!
DORIAN! ARE YOU OKAY?!
SIGH...
EVERYTHING WAS BETTER BEFORE.

DORIAN AND I ONLY HAD EACH OTHER.

WE DIDN'T NEED ANYTHING ELSE!

HE WAS SO CLUMSY AND STUBBORN AND FUNNY.

HE NEEDED ME.

WHERE'S DANI?
I DON'T KNOW.

HERE'S YOUR JACKET, MARK.
DANI WAS WEARING THAT!

GUYS... I THINK I KNOW WHERE DANI IS...
SHE FOUND MONICA.

WHERE ARE THEY?!

!

OH...

CHAPTER 37

HOW DID YOU FIND ME?
DID YOU FOLLOW THE BIRDS?
WHERE IS EVERYONE?
DANI, ARE YOU OKAY?
...
I HAD A FIGHT WITH DORIAN.
OH... WHY?

HE...HE GOT VIOLENT, AND...I DON'T KNOW. IT ISN'T RIGHT.

I GAVE HER THE POTION I MADE WITH DORIAN.
LET'S SEE IF IT WORKED!

LITTLE GIRL...WHERE ARE YOU?
AH, SHE WOKE UP!

DID MY AMAZING POTION WORK?

LITTLE GIRL...WHAT HAVE YOU DONE?
AH! WHAT IS...?!

YOUR POTION IS IMPRESSIVE!

A MONSTER!!
MONICA, MOVE, I WILL—!
DANI, SHE'S A HARMLESS OLD LADY!
HUH?
BUT...

MY POTION DIDN'T WORK. YOU STILL LOOK HORR...
I MEAN, LIKE A WOLF.
THAT'S THE LEAST OF MY WORRIES, SWEETHEART.

I FEEL GREAT! MY BONES DON'T HURT ANYMORE!
LOOK, I CAN EVEN DANCE!
REALLY??
MY POTION WORKED, THEN!
THIS IS SO WEIRD...

PLEASE GIVE ME THE RECIPE FOR THAT POTION. I'D BE SO GRATEFUL.
OF COURSE!
WHO WOULD HAVE THOUGHT WITCHES COULD BE USEFUL...

DID YOU HEAR THAT, DANI?
WE CONVINCED HER THAT WITCHES AREN'T EVIL! AND WITH A SIMPLE POTION.

THAT'S TRUE!
WE COULD MAKE A BUNCH AND DISTRIBUTE IT TO PEOPLE.
WE'LL PROVE THAT WITCHES CAN DO GOOD!

BUT YOU AND THE OLD LADY BETTER DO IT...
I MIGHT TURN THE POTION INTO POISON.

YOU'RE THE MOST POWERFUL WITCH HERE—YOU SHOULDN'T JUST WATCH!
ALL THREE OF US WILL MAKE IT.
WAIT—

BY THE WAY, EARLIER YOU WERE TELLING ME ABOUT YOUR FIGHT WITH DORIAN.

ARE YOU FEELING BETTER?

I DON'T KNOW...
MY HEAD'S A MESS AND THE DISTANCE BETWEEN DORIAN AND ME HAS WIDENED...
MAYBE IT'S SILLY, BUT...
I FEEL LONELY. AND A BIT SAD. NOT ALL THE TIME. BUT WAY MORE THAN I USED TO.

THAT'S NORMAL, DANI.
SO MUCH HAS HAPPENED. SOME REALLY BAD THINGS.

BUT YOU CAN'T KEEP EVERYTHING TO YOURSELF.
WHEN YOU TRY TO SOLVE PROBLEMS ALONE, THEY GET BIGGER AND GROW INWARD.
THEY GET STUCK IN YOUR SOUL...
TRUST OTHERS FOR HELP. WE'RE HERE. NOT JUST DORIAN, EVERYBODY.

YOU'RE RIGHT, MONICA. IS THAT WHY YOU'RE ALWAYS NAGGING US??
OF COURSE! CAN'T YOU SEE HOW WELL IT'S WORKING FOR ME?
...
CAN'T YOU??
HA-HA, OF COURSE. ACTUALLY, THERE'S SOMETHING I SHOULD GET OUT...
BUT IT'S EMBARRASSING....
WHAT IS IT?

I WAS... I AM...
A BIT JEALOUS OF YOU.

OF ME? WHY??
I DON'T KNOW... DORIAN'S SO FOND OF YOU...
THERE'S SOMETHING BETWEEN YOU.
WHAT?!

NOT AT ALL, DANI!
YOU'RE COMPLETELY WRONG!
TELL ME.
WE'RE FRIENDS.
AND NOT EVEN AS CLOSE AS YOU THINK.
REALLY?
OF COURSE! HA, WHAT AN IDEA. I'M MARRYING WILL, YOU KNOW THAT.
FOOD IS READY!
WE'VE TRACKED THEM THIS FAR—
WAIT, LOOK IN THAT WINDOW!
IS THAT...A WOLF?
IT'S A MONSTER!
LET'S GO KICK ITS BUTT!
YES, LET'S DO IT.

ATTACK!
YOU'LL BE SORRY, WOLF!
DID YOU HEAR THAT?
WAS IT—?
GIRLS, WOULD YOU RATHER HAVE CHEESECAKE OR FRUIT SAL—?
BOOM
GRANNY!!
WE KNOW YOU'VE KIDNAPPED MY SISTER AND THE PRINCESS!
WHERE ARE THEY?!
TELL US OR YOU'LL BE SORRY!
HUH...?!
HEY!
KIDS THESE DAYS ARE SO IMPOLITE.

ASK BEFORE ATTACKING!
SHE'S JUST A CURSED OLD LADY.
APOLOGIZE RIGHT NOW!

I'M SO SORRY, MADAM...
CLEAN THIS UP!

MONICA, YOU'RE SAFE!

YOU BOTH ARE! WE FOUND YOU THANKS TO DANI.
DON'T TOUCH THE PRINCESS WITH YOUR SWEATY HANDS!

YOU HUGGED HER JUST NOW TOO, IVY.
I SHOWER REGULARLY.
ARE YOU HUNGRY?

HUH...
NOW THAT YOU MENTION IT...
DANI... ARE YOU STILL ANGRY?

I'M SORRY.
I WAS NERVOUS...AND SCARED.

HA, WHAT ARE YOU TALKING ABOUT?
UGH!

YOU'RE SO SILLY, DORIAN.
IT'S OKAY. I WAS SCARED, TOO.

SERIOUSLY, IT'S OKAY.

OOH, A YOUNG MAN WITH A BIG APPETITE!
IT'S JUST THAT EVERYTHING IS SO DELICIOUS, MADAM!

YOU CAN CALL ME GRANNY, SON!

I'D LOVE TO HAVE A GRANDCHILD AS CUTE AS YOU!

MONICA...
WOW, YOU'RE FINALLY SAYING HELLO.
I THOUGHT YOU DIDN'T REMEMBER ME.

CAN I HUG YOU?
...HUH?

WE...
OF COURSE! THE OTHERS ALREADY DID! WHY ARE YOU SO AWKWARD?
DON'T ASK IT SO SERIOUSLY OR IT'S GONNA BE MORE AWKWARD!

...

...PHEW.

W... WHAT?
I WAS SCARED...
WHEN YOU FELL FROM THE VAN...

I'M GLAD YOU'RE OKAY.
HA-HA, DON'T YOU TRUST ME?

OF COURSE I DO, BUT HOW COULD I NOT WORRY?

I'M YOUR BOYFRIEND, AFTER ALL.

WHAT?!

WHERE DID YOU GET THAT IDEA?

HUH...?
WHEN WE WERE AT THE CASTLE I TOLD YOU I LIKED YOU...

AND YOU...YOU TOLD ME THAT YOU DIDN'T DISLIKE ME. REMEMBER?
YES, BUT...

INTENSE...
OH, YOU POOR WRETCH.

THERE'S A BIG DIFFERENCE BETWEEN SAYING THAT I DON'T DISLIKE YOU AND AGREEING TO BE YOUR GIRLFRIEND!
HAVE YOU SERIOUSLY THOUGHT WE WERE A COUPLE ALL THIS TIME?!

AH... I...
THAT'S IMPOSSIBLE!
I'M ENGAGED TO WILLIAM! REMEMBER?

...

HA...
YEAH, OF COURSE. I'M SORRY.
WAIT—
IT DOESN'T MATTER.

IT'S JUST THAT I THOUGHT...
NEVER MIND.

I'M...I'M GOING OUTSIDE FOR A SECOND.

DORIAN, HANG ON!
LET HIM GO!

I THINK I SCREWED UP...
YOU DIDN'T SCREW ANYTHING UP, PRINCESS.
IT WAS THE RIGHT THING TO SET THE RECORD STRAIGHT!

SOMEONE SHOULD GO TALK TO HIM.
HUH? WHY ME?

HELP ME POUR THE POTION INTO THE VIALS!
WHAT POTION?
IT'S MEDICINE THE THREE OF US MADE.
IT'S GOOD FOR MILD ACHES AND PAINS BUT IS ALSO AN ANTIDOTE TO SOME POISONS.

WE'RE GONNA PUT TWO STAMPS ON THEM:

THE ROYAL STAMP, WHICH BELONGS TO MONICA'S FAMILY...

AND THE ONE THAT REPRESENTS WITCHES,
TO PROVE THAT WITCHES CAN GET ALONG WITH THE REST OF THE WORLD!
WHOA, THAT'S A REALLY GOOD IDEA!

DO WE REALLY HAVE TO DRESS IN BLACK?
I DON'T WANT TO LOOK LIKE A WITCH.
YOU LOOK GOOD, IVY.
DANI, WAIT!

DORIAN...
ARE YOU OKAY?

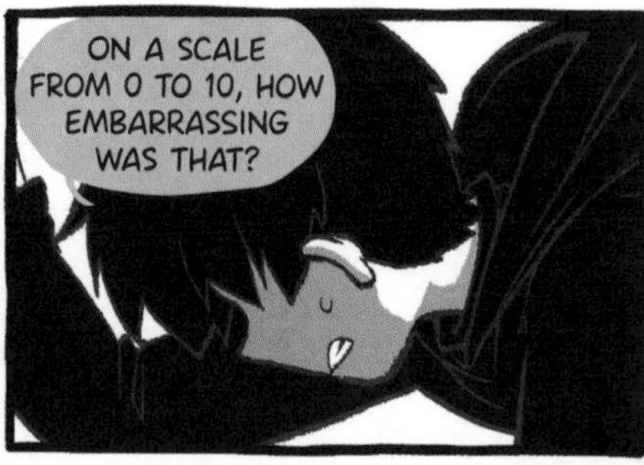
ON A SCALE FROM 0 TO 10, HOW EMBARRASSING WAS THAT?

BE HONEST.
FROM 0 TO 10...?
MAYBE 8 AND A HALF.
...I WANT TO DIE.
COME ON, DON'T SAY THAT...
HOW WILL I EVEN LOOK AT HER NOW?
BUT...DO YOU REALLY EVEN LIKE MONICA?

OF COURSE! I LIKE HER SO MUCH!
STOP IT! I'M EMBARRASSED JUST LISTENING TO YOU!
DO YOU THINK I HAVE ANY CHANCE? SHE SAID SHE DOESN'T DISLIKE ME.
WE'RE CLEAR ON THAT.

CHEER UP—
NO WAY!

WHAT DID YOU TELL ME A COUPLE OF MONTHS AGO, DORIAN? OH... RIGHT.
"I DON'T UNDERSTAND WHAT'S SO FUN ABOUT THESE STUPID ROMANTIC THINGS. AND AREN'T YOU A BIT TOO YOUNG TO DATE?"
WASN'T THAT YOU?
WELL... YES, BUT—

STICK TO YOUR WORDS, THEN!
WE HAVE MORE IMPORTANT THINGS TO DO!
FIRST: DISTRIBUTE THE POTION.
SECOND: FIND WILLIAM.

RIGHT. IT'S ALWAYS ABOUT WILLIAM...
THIRD: BRING DAMIEN OVER TO OUR SIDE.
AND FOURTH: MAKE MOM AND DAD SEE SENSE.

OH, THERE YOU ARE.
THERE'S NO TIME FOR ROMANCE.

ROMANCE IS FORBIDDEN UNTIL FURTHER NOTICE.
ALL ROMANCE...?

WE HAVE A MISSION TO FULFILL!
!,
DANI, LET ME GO.

AH...
DORIAN, LISTEN—

HEY, GUYS!

LET'S GO!
WE HAVE A LOT OF WORK TO DO!

CHAPTER 38

I SWEAR, MRS. WYTTE. IT WAS PRINCESS MONICA!
AND WE'RE ALMOST SURE THAT THE OTHER KIDS WERE DANIELA AND DORIAN WYTTE.

THESE KIDS ARE GETTING OUT OF CONTROL.
SOLDIERS!
SPREAD THE WORD.

WANTED
EACH SQUAD MUST HAVE A WITCH WITH THEM.

WE NEED TO FIND MY NIECE AND NEPHEW.

WANTED
WANTED
WANTED
WANTED
WANTED
WE CAN'T SPEND ONE MORE DAY WITHOUT THEM ON OUR SIDE!

IF YOU SEE ANY OF THESE KIDS AROUND HERE...
YOU HAVE TO NOTIFY THE AUTHORITIES.

IS THERE A REWARD?
YOU'RE WITCHES. YOU OWE YOUR LOYALTY TO KING DAMIEN.

HAVE A NICE DAY.
DING DONG
BAH!

NOW 50%
Alice &
NO REWARD?
WE'RE NOT BABYSITTERS FOR THOSE SNOBBY WYTTES.

THOSE POSTERS ARE A BUMMER!
GOING UNNOTICED HAS BEEN DIFFICULT LATELY.
YAWN...
THIS IS EXHAUSTING.
DON'T YOU DARE FALL ASLEEP WHILE DRIVING!
AAAH!
I'M SORRY!
LOOK. MAYBE WE CAN FIND AN INN IN THIS TOWN.
OR SOMEONE WHO'D LET US STAY WITH THEM.
IMPOSSIBLE.
AS SOON AS THEY SEE US, THEY'LL CALL DAMIEN'S ARMY.
THEN WHAT DO YOU SUGGEST, COUNTRY BOY?
NOT ALL OF US ENJOY SLEEPING IN A STINKY VAN OR THE MIDDLE OF A MUDDY FOREST LIKE YOU.
LEAVE IT TO ME.
PERFECT.

IF IT WOULD BE POSSIBLE TO SPEND THE NIGHT AT YOUR HOUSE, SIR.

...

OH... I SEE...

NO PROBLEM.

COME IN, COME IN!

ALICE, LOOK WHO IS HERE...

OUR FIRST STUDENTS!
OH! SO YOU'RE INTERESTED IN DARK MAGIC?
YOU'VE COME TO THE RIGHT PLACE. WELCOME!
WE'RE ACTUALLY MORE INTERESTED IN DINNER.
OF COURSE.
YOU CAN ALSO TAKE OFF THOSE COSTUMES.
HUH? HOW DO YOU KNOW THAT WE'RE IN COSTUME?
HOW OLD ARE YOU? 12?
13!
WHATEVER. THAT GRAY MUSTACHE DOESN'T LOOK VERY CONVINCING!
BY THE WAY, I'M ALICE. AND HE'S ROMAS.
NOW 50%
Alice &
DISCOUNTS FOR GROUP

MAKE YOURSELVES COMFORTABLE.
I'M GOING TO MAKE THE BEST SPAGHETTI CARBONARA YOU'VE EVER TASTED.
THANK YOU!

IT SEEMS WE HAVE HAD A STROKE OF LUCK, ROMAS!
I DON'T KNOW...
REMEMBER THAT THERE'S NO REWARD FOR FINDING THE WYTTE KIDS.

STILL...
MAYBE WE CAN GET SOMETHING OUT OF ALL THIS.

THAT'S WHAT I WANT TO FIND OUT.
WHAT IS HAPPENING WITH THIS FAMILY...
AND HOW CAN WE TAKE ADVANTAGE OF IT?
THERE YOU GO. I HOPE YOU ENJOY IT.
EAT UP AND THEN GO UP TO THE SECOND FLOOR. THIRD DOOR ON THE LEFT.
YOU CAN SLEEP THERE.
HURRY UP THOUGH.
SOME OF THE SPIRITS WHO INHABIT THIS HOUSE CAN BE ODD AND HOSTILE.
A DECENT MEAL AT LAST. I WAS SICK OF MARK'S SOUPS.
IT LOOKS YUMMY!
HEY!
ODD SPIRITS...?
GOSH... GLAD TO HEAR THAT.
GOOD NIGHT.
I'M ACTUALLY EXCITED ABOUT THIS!
IT'S LIKE A REAL-LIFE HORROR STORY.
I THOUGHT YOU LOVED THOSE, NICO!
YEAH, WELL...

NOW THAT WE HAVE SOME RESPITE, THERE'S SOMETHING I NEED TO TELL YOU.
EVERYONE ELSE KNOWS.
WELL, EXCEPT FOR DORIAN. I DIDN'T KNOW HOW HE WOULD REACT.
HUH? TO WHAT?
YOU ALREADY KNOW WHAT I THINK...
WHAT ARE YOU TALKING ABOUT, NICO...?
I THINK YOU SHOULDN'T COME WITH US.
?
THIS COULD BE DANGEROUS.
WHAT DO YOU MEAN?
DANI KNOWS WHAT I MEAN. DON'T YOU, DANI?
THERE'S SOMETHING WRONG WITH YOU.
EVERYTHING YOU DO HARMS PEOPLE.
YOU'RE THE QUEEN OF WI—
SHUT YOUR MOUTH!
YOU KNOW THAT I'M NOT A BAD PERSON!
I ONLY WANT PEOPLE TO ACCEPT WITCHES!

SLAP
CALM DOWN, DANI!
WE BELIEVE YOU'RE A GOOD PERSON, DON'T MAKE US CHANGE OUR MINDS.

BUT IT'S EVIDENT THAT YOU'RE A DANGER TO EVERYONE.
WE'RE NOT GONNA HURT YOU, BUT YOU NEED TO STAY OUT OF THINGS!

BUT, MONICA—

DON'T TOUCH ME!
DON'T TOUCH HER!

DANI, WHAT THEY'RE SAYING MAKES SENSE.
YOU CAN'T EVEN CAST A SPELL WITHOUT HARMING SOMEONE.
YOU'RE THE QUEEN OF WITCHES.
NO...! WHAT ARE YOU...?
AND YOU'VE BEEN VERY AGGRESSIVE LATELY.
WHY CAN'T YOU JUST BE LIKE THE OLD DANI?
WHY AREN'T YOU LIKE THE OLD DORIAN?
THE OLD DORIAN NO LONGER EXISTS.
WHY ARE YOU DOING THIS TO ME?
SHE'S TELLING THE TRUTH.
IT DOESN'T EXIST BECAUSE NONE OF THIS IS TRUE.
WHAT?
WAKE UP, DANI.

THIS IS JUST YOUR IMAGINATION.
HUH?
WHERE...?
WHERE AM I?
WHAT IS THIS?
NICO?
MARK?
...
...ALEX?
HAVE I BEEN DREAMING ALL OF THIS?
THIS IS REAL, I'M SURE OF IT...

IT CAN'T BE...
WHERE IS EVERYONE, THEN?
AM I BACK AT THE CASTLE? IN A TOWER?
HOW MANY STAIRS ARE THERE?
HOW LONG HAVE I BEEN CLIMBING?

IT MUST BE THE SPIRITS...
THEY'RE PLAYING TRICKS ON ME!

THIRD DOOR ON THE LEFT...

IF I GET INSIDE THE ROOM I'M SURE...!

JUST IN TIME...
YOUR DINNER IS SERVED...
...YOUR MAJESTY.

WHAT...?
WHAT IS THIS?

WHERE AM I?

LOOKS LIKE SHE'S NOT DOING VERY WELL.
EATING WILL HELP. YOU'LL FEEL BETTER, YOUR MAJESTY!

WHAT HAVE YOU DONE?
WHERE'S MY BROTHER?
WHERE'S DORIAN?

DON'T YOU REMEMBER?

YOUR BROTHER IS NO LONGER HERE, YOUR MAJESTY.
IT'S BEEN YEARS...

STOP LYING!

WAIT!
THIRD DOOR ON THE LEFT...

NO...
WHERE AM I?
I NEED TO GET OUT OF HERE...
DANI! ARE YOU OK?
...DORIAN?
ARE YOU REAL?
I DON'T KNOW. ARE YOU?

YES. AT LEAST I THINK SO... CAN YOU REMEMBER ANYTHING?

W-WE'RE GOING TO FIND PRINCE WILLIAM, AND RESCUE HIM...

WE WANTED TO GIVE OUT THOSE HEALING POTIONS ALONG THE WAY...
TO MAKE PEOPLE TRUST MAGIC.
REALLY?
YEAH.
THAT'S... REALLY NICE.
THEY'RE HEALING POTIONS, THEN...
I FEEL A BIT SORRY.
WE COULD USE THAT, ALICE...

MAYBE WE'VE GONE TOO FAR.
THAT'S NOT OUR FAULT.

IT'S THE HOUSE'S SPIRIT MAKING THEM LIVE THEIR WORST NIGHTMARES.

CHAPTER 39

KNOCK
KNOCK

I'M HERE TO DELIVER YOUR ORDER FROM EVAN'S CAFÉ!
COMING!

YOU GOT HERE SO FAST, MARK.
WHO ARE YOU, MADAM?

WHAT ARE YOU TALKING ABOUT? I'M MRS. GERTRUDIS, MARK.
GERTRUDIS...? BUT...
HOW ABOUT PENDRAGON? AND...NICO?
WHO?

Gertrudis Haberdashery
THIS IS WHERE PENDRAGON USED TO DIVINE PEOPLE'S FUTURE WITH HIS MAGIC!
...MAGIC?

NICO...?
IT DOESN'T RING A BELL.
WITCHES AND FORTUNE-TELLERS? HAVE YOU SLEPT?
BUT, DA—

MAGIC DOESN'T EXIST.
I DIDN'T MAKE IT ALL UP! OF COURSE THEY EXIST!
PENDRAGON EXISTS! AND NICO!

HEY, DUDE!
ARE YOU OK?
WHERE AM I? NICO?
IT'S ME—YOU HALLUCINATED.
I THINK THEY HEXED US OR SOMETHING...
REALLY? IT SEEMED SO REAL...
WHAT DID YOU SEE?
NEVER MIND.
WE NEED TO FIND EVERYONE ELSE BEFORE THEIR NIGHTMARES TAKE OVER.

NO...
THIS CAN'T BE...

I KNOW IT'S TOO LATE, BUT... THE TRUTH IS, I ALWAYS...

I'VE ALWAYS LOVED—
HEY!
COME ON! THINGS WERE JUST GETTING INTERESTING.
WHAT A SHAME.
OOPS, SORRY.

COME ON, MONICA...
WHAT WERE YOU SEEING?
WE HAVEN'T GOT TIME FOR THIS. WE NEED TO FIND THE TWINS AS SOON AS WE CAN.
KNOWING THEM...
THEY'RE HAVING TERRIBLE NIGHTMARES.

DANI!
WHERE ARE YOU GOING?
NO!

DANI!
WAIT!

CAREFUL, DORIAN!
HUH...?
THAT WAS CLOSE, DUDE!

WHAT...?
YOU ALMOST JUMPED.
HOW SCARY...
LUCKILY WE GOT HERE IN TIME!

I REMEMBER NOW...
WHERE'S DANI?
WE STILL HAVEN'T FOUND HER.
BUT WE'VE FOUND THOSE TWO.

LOOK!
FREE POTIONS!
Alice & Romas Witchcraft Academy
TRY THEM OUT, NO CHARGE!
Potions of a thousand uses!
ENROL TODAY!
A HOMEMADE CREATION OF THE WITCHCRAFT ACADEMY BY ALICE AND ROMAS!

OUR POTIONS!

HEY, WAIT. THAT'S...

I'M COMING, DANI!!

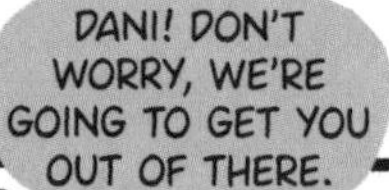

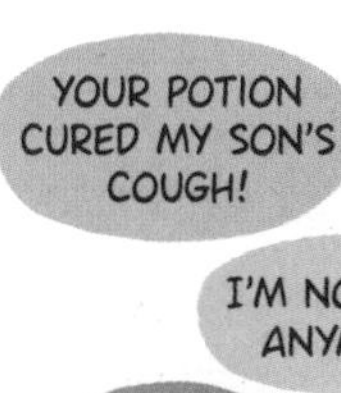
YOUR POTION CURED MY SON'S COUGH!

IT UNBLOCKED THE DRAIN!
I'M NOT BALD ANYMORE!
IT'S A POTION OF A THOUSAND USES!
YOU'LL LEARN HOW TO DO THIS AND MORE BY ENROLLING IN OUR ACADEMY.
I WANT TO ENROLL!
HERE'S ANOTHER SUBSCRIPTION LIST! HURRY UP, THERE ARE LIMITED PLACES AVAILABLE!
ME TOO!

DARN IT.
THAT WAS DANI'S IDEA!
WELL...IT WORKED.
ARE YOU ALL RIGHT?
AND THEY *ARE* MAKING PEOPLE TRUST WITCHES, RIGHT?
AT THE END OF THE DAY, THEY'RE BECOMING FAMILIAR WITH MAGIC. RIGHT?

...

MONICA...
I NEED TO TALK TO YOU...

WHAT?

WHAT DO YOU WANT TO TELL ME...?
WELL...

THIS IS HARD...
I KNOW WHAT'S HAPPENING!
YOU HAD A NIGHTMARE ABOUT ME, RIGHT? WHEN WE WERE UNDER THAT SPELL?

NO, NO! IT'S NOTHING LIKE THAT!

WHAT I WANTED TO TELL YOU IS...

WHAT I SAID ABOUT LIKING YOU... WELL, ALL OF THAT. FORGET ABOUT IT.
...WHAT?
WHY?

I'VE THOUGHT ABOUT IT AND...I WAS WRONG!
I DON'T REALLY LIKE YOU THAT MUCH, YOU KNOW? IT'S NOT THAT SERIOUS.
YOU'RE THE FIRST GIRL I'VE EVER MET AFTER ALL, EXCEPT FOR MY FAMILY AND MY BABYSITTER.

IS THAT SO?
YES, DON'T WORRY ABOUT IT.

I HAD TO TELL YOU SO YOU WOULDN'T FEEL UNCOMFORTABLE AROUND ME.
WE CAN GO ON AS IF NOTHING HAPPENED AND STILL BE FRIENDS.
YEAH...SURE, FRIENDS.
JUST A SILLY MISUNDERSTANDING, THEN.
YES.
AHH!!
AAAARGH!
WHOA...!
EVERYBODY TURNED INTO WOLVES?!
UGH! LEAVE ME ALONE!
AND CARNIVOROUS PLANTS?!

HOW IS THIS POSSIBLE?
HOW?

BECAUSE DANI MADE THE POTIONS, OF COURSE!

I'VE FINALLY FOUND YOU.

IT WAS YOU, WASN'T IT?
INDEED...
WAS ANY OF THAT REAL?
THE FIGHT WITH MY FRIENDS?
DORIAN'S DISAPPEARANCE?
ME BEING THE QUEEN?
WHO KNOWS?
WHAT IS REAL?
YOU DID ALL THIS TO SCARE ME, DIDN'T YOU? WHY?
HOW DO YOU KNOW ME SO WELL?
I KNOW EVERYTHING ABOUT FEAR AND PAIN.
AND...I SIMPLY DO AS I AM TOLD.
BY WHOM? ALICE AND ROMAS?
WHY THEM?
I FEED OFF OF EVIL...
GET ME OUT OF HERE.
NO.
YOU'VE SCARED ME ENOUGH ALREADY.
WHAT ELSE DO YOU WANT?
I OBEY.

WELL, OBEY ME, THEN.

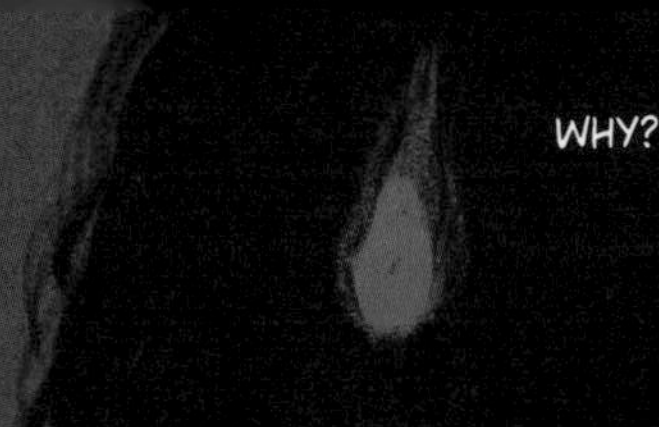
WHY?

BECAUSE I'M WAY MORE EVIL THAN THOSE TWO.
YOU'LL BE BETTER OFF WITH ME.
NO, YOU'RE NOT...
YOU'RE A GOOD KID. I CAN TELL.

ARE YOU SURE?
TAKE A CLOSER LOOK.

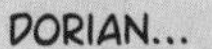

WHAT ARE YOU DOING?

ALL RIGHT...
FOR NOW.
HUH?!
WHAT THE HECK IS GOING ON?!
LOOK, SOMEONE'S CATCHING THE WOLVES!
HOW IS THIS POSSIBLE?
WHAT THE...?
OH...
GOOD JOB, SPIRIT!
WHO'S—
DANI?!
HOW DID YOU DO THAT?!

THERE'S NO TIME TO EXPLAIN.
WE NEED TO TURN EVERYONE BACK TO NORMAL!
COME ON, DORIAN!
WHOA!

YOU DO KNOW THE RIGHT WAY TO MAKE THAT POTION, DON'T YOU?
YOU TOO, MONICA.
HURRY UP!
YES...
DANI, ANSWER MY QUESTION!

HOW'S EVERYTHING GOING?

THE QUANTITY OF PEOPLE AFFECTED BY THE POTION IS INCREASING.
DON'T WORRY, THOUGH. I'VE GOT THIS.
THANK YOU, SPIRIT!

LET'S GO DORIAN.
YES!
SPIRIT? WHAT SPIRIT? ARE YOU TALKING TO YOUR CAT?
YOU'RE COMING WITH ME, MONICA. PEOPLE NEED TO SEE YOU.
ALL RIGHT!

GET OUT OF THE WAY, EVERYONE...
WHOAA!
LOOK AT THE SKY!
IS THAT A BUBBLE?
TAKE COVER! THEY WANT TO TURN US ALL INTO WOLVES!
AND NOW...
EXPLODE!
HUH...?
AAAARGH!
RUN!
HELP!
THE CAGES
DISSOLVING
WHAT
HAPPENE

I TURNED INTO A WOLF?!
BUT YOU WERE SO CUTE! WITH SHARP TEETH AND POINTY EARS!
WHO CHANGED ME BACK?
THEY DID!
ISN'T THAT PRINCESS MONICA?!
AND AREN'T THEY THE WYTTE KIDS?
YES!
WANTED
THEY SAVED US! THEY MUST BE GOOD WITCHES.

THE OTHERS, THOUGH...
THEY CURSED US!
CATCH THEM!

YOU'LL BE SORRY!

THEY GOT AWAY...
MRS. WYTTE IS GONNA KILL US.

INTERROGATE THOSE OTHER WITCHES THOROUGHLY. WE'LL SEE IF THEY KNOW WHERE THE KIDS ARE HEADED.
WANTED

THE PRIORITY RIGHT NOW IS TO CAPTURE THE RUNAWAYS.

WHAT HAPPENED HERE...?
THAT'S TO BE EXPECTED WHEN YOU STICK YOUR NOSE INTO SHADY MATTERS, PENDRAGON.
BUT YOU SET ME FREE.
ARE YOU ON THE GOOD SIDE NOW?
IS THERE SUCH A THING? I SET YOU FREE BECAUSE I NEED SOMETHING FROM YOU.
YOU NEED MY HELP TO FIND PRINCE WILLIAM.
CORRECT. CAN YOU DO IT OR NOT?
YES, I CAN TRY TO FIND HIM WITH MY CRYSTAL BALL.
BUT I WONDER...
WHY DIDN'T YOU ASK YOUR PARENTS DIRECTLY?
... ARE YOU STUP—?
I MEAN, YOU DON'T NEED TO MENTION THAT YOU WANT TO SAVE HIM!
YOU'RE THE KING, IT WOULDN'T BE STRANGE IF YOU HAD ACCESS TO IMPORTANT INFORMATION.
MY MOTHER WOULDN'T BUY IT.
SHE KNOWS ME TOO WELL.
IS IT THAT OBVIOUS?
WHY DO YOU CARE SO MUCH ABOUT THAT BOY?
WHY, YOU ASK?
WELL...

CHAPTER 40

MY MOM HAD CHANGED.

HER GENTLENESS HAD TURNED INTO BITTERNESS.

ALL SHE SOUGHT WAS VENGEANCE...

AND EVERYONE ELSE WAS PLAYING ALONG.

WE NEED THE MAGICAL COMMUNITY ON OUR SIDE.

MANY OF THEM DON'T WANT ANYTHING TO DO WITH US. THEY'RE ON GOOD TERMS WITH THE KING.

THAT'S TRUE, BUT IF WE'RE WILLING TO WAIT A WHILE...

WE COULD TRAIN THE NEXT GENERATION OF WITCHES. SHOW THEM OUR CAUSE.

AND HOW ARE YOU PLANNING TO DO THAT?

A SCHOOL.

FOR ALL WITCHES?

THAT'S RIGHT, HILDE.

FOR ALL THE YOUNG WITCHES LIVING IN THE KINGDOM.

WHAT...?!
WHAT ARE YOU DOING HERE? WHERE DID YOU COME FROM?!
DO IT AGAIN!
HUH...?! DO WHAT?!
MAGIC! YOU WERE MAKING TOADS AND SNAKES.
DO IT AGAIN!
YOU'RE CONFUSED. THAT'S IMPOSSIBLE.
OH, SURE!
I KNOW WHAT YOU ARE.
WHAT?!
WHAT I...?
OF COURSE,
YOU ARE...
I AM...
IT'S THE FIRST TIME I'VE MET ONE...
YOU'RE...
A GNOME!

HOW ON EARTH DO *I* LOOK LIKE A GNOME?
LIKE A GARDEN GNOME. HOW COOL!
I'M NOT YOUR GARDEN GNOME!!

I WON'T TELL ANYONE! IT'LL BE OUR SECRET.
MY NAME'S DAMIEN. I'M NOT A GNOME.

WILLIAM!
PRINCE WILLIAM!
WHERE ARE YOU?!
OH.
PRINCE?!

AH, THEY'RE LOOKING FOR ME.
I NEED TO GO, LITTLE GNOME!
IT'S DAMIEN.
WE'LL MEET HERE TOMORROW, OK?
DON'T TELL ANYONE YOU SAW ME!

I DON'T WANT HIM TO GO TO THAT SCHOOL.
WHY NOT, ANGELA?

HE'LL BE HAPPIER HERE, AT HOME.
SAFE.
THE SCHOOL COULD HELP HIM SEE OUR SIDE. HE'S BEEN GROWING DISTANT.

HAVING SOMEONE ACCEPT ME WAS EXTREMELY GRATIFYING, EVEN THOUGH HE DIDN'T KNOW WHO I REALLY WAS.

IN TRUTH, IT WAS SURPRISINGLY EASY. WE BECAME FRIENDS.

WE PLAYED IN SECRET. MY PARENTS COULDN'T FIND OUT THAT I LET SOMEONE NONMAGICAL GET CLOSE TO ME.

WILLIAM THOUGHT THAT SECRETLY PLAYING WITH A FOREST GNOME WAS AN ADVENTURE.

HE SAW
HIMSELF AS
THE HERO OF
A TALE.
IT ALL CAME
NATURALLY.
UNTIL ONE
DAY HE NEVER
CAME BACK.

AND I WAS
LEFT LONELIER
THAN EVER.
I GOT OUT OF THAT
FAIRY TALE AND BACK INTO
THE REAL WORLD, WHERE
MY FURIOUS PARENTS WERE
PLANNING TO DESTROY
EVERYTHING.
AND OF COURSE,
I DIDN'T HAVE ANY
FRIENDS.

DAD,
MOM.
I WANT
TO GO TO
SCHOOL.
SO I MADE
A DECISION.

...

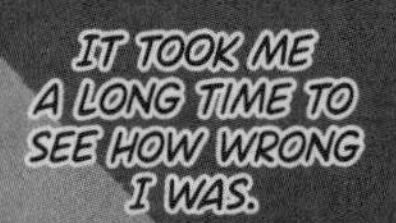
IT TOOK ME A LONG TIME TO SEE HOW WRONG I WAS.

TEACHERS TRIED THEIR BEST TO INSTILL HATE IN OUR HEARTS.

THEY CENSOR US, THEY PERSECUTE US, THEY KILL US. THEY THINK THEY CAN JUDGE—

HURRY, NOAH!

COME ON, GUYS, WHAT'S THE MATTER? CHEER UP!
ALEX! GET DOWN RIGHT NOW!
NOAH AND BARRY, YOU TOO!
BUT, PROFESSOR...

...

I DON'T WANT TO GO THERE EVER AGAIN...
I'LL TELL MOM... SHE'LL LET ME STAY AT HOME.

ALL OF THIS STARTED BECAUSE OF ME.

HEY...
HELLO, GARDEN GNOME.
...!
GET OUT OF MY WAY OR I'LL TURN YOU INTO—!

...WILL?
LONG TIME NO SEE, DAMIEN!

I...
I WASN'T CRYING! DON'T GET ANY IDEAS!
CRYING? I DIDN'T SEE ANYTHING.

...
WHERE HAVE YOU BEEN?

...SO NOW I'M LIVING AT MY FIANCÉE'S PALACE.
MY FATHER OWED HER FATHER A FAVOR, SO IT'S MY DUTY TO MARRY MONICA.
WHOA...

I CAME FOR A VISIT, BUT I NEED TO GET BACK TOMORROW.
WHAT? YOU'RE NOT STAYING?

I CAN'T.

...
LISTEN...
MH?
DO YOU WANNA COME WITH ME?

WHAT?
IT'D BE SO COOL!
YOU COULD TEACH ME HOW TO DO MAGIC!

WILL...THERE'S SOMETHING I NEED TO TELL YOU...

YOU CAN'T LIE TO WILL FOREVER. ACCEPT THAT YOU'RE ON YOUR OWN.

WHAT THE HELL ARE YOU THINKING?
THAT'S TOO DANGEROUS, DAMIEN.
BUT I'LL BE AT THE CASTLE, UNDERCOVER...
THAT COULD HELP WITH YOUR PLAN.
SWEETHEART, THAT'S NOT NECESSARY.
PRINCE WILLIAM TRUSTS ME, NOBODY WILL SUSPECT A THING.
...JUST COME RIGHT BACK IF ANYTHING SEEMS OFF.
YES, DAD.
AND COME HOME FOR CHRISTMAS AND YOUR BIRTHDAY, DAMIEN.
I PROMISE, MOM.
IT WAS THE ONLY WAY THEY WOULD ALLOW ME TO JOIN WILL.
HERE WE ARE!

AND THAT'S HOW MY LIFE AT THE PALACE BEGAN.

IT WAS SUCH A LIVELY PLACE...

FULL OF KIDS MY AGE TO PLAY WITH.

I KNEW THAT I DIDN'T HAVE HIS STATUS,

UGH...I HAVE A TUMMY ACHE...
?

BUT WILL MADE ME FEEL LIKE I DID.

THAT KEPT MY PARENTS CALM AND ALLOWED ME TO LIVE MY LIFE AT THE PALACE IN PEACE.

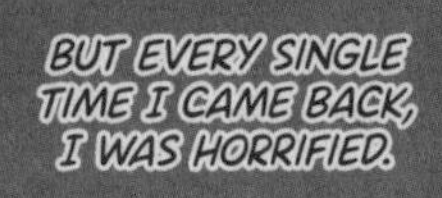

THEIR FANTASIES OF VENGEANCE WERE ONLY INCREASING.

TIME WAS FLYING BY...
AND I WAS BEGINNING TO REALIZE WHERE I BELONGED AND WHICH SIDE I WAS ON.
I KNEW IT.
YOUR MAJESTY...!
WHAT ARE YOU DOING HERE?
WHY HAVE YOU KEPT THIS FROM ME FOR SO MANY YEARS, DAMIEN?
I...I DIDN'T...
WHAT ARE YOU AFRAID OF?
YOUR MAJESTY, PLEASE, I MEANT NO HARM... I...
I AM NOT WHO I USED TO BE, DAMIEN.
HUH?

I'M NOT AFRAID OF YOUR KIND ANYMORE.
COME ON, DAMIEN, LOOK AT ME. I TRUST YOU.
I KNOW YOU'RE A GOOD PERSON.

...
...
...
THANK YOU, YOUR MAJESTY.
WOULD YOU LIKE TO BE MY PERSONAL BUTLER, DAMIEN?
SOMEONE LIKE YOU COULD BE VERY USEFUL TO THE CROWN.
...WHAT?!

DON'T TELL ANYONE YOU'RE A WITCH THOUGH.
DAMIEN, WE NEED YOU TO BRING PRINCE WILLIAM TO US.

YOU'RE FAMILIAR WITH HIM, AREN'T YOU?
IT WON'T BE TOO HARD.
WHAT?
WHAT DO YOU NEED HIM FOR?
THERE'S NO BETTER HOSTAGE THAN A CROWN PRINCE. WE'LL KIDNAP ALL OF THEM.
...DAMIEN?
THIS IS AN ABSURD PLAN.
CAN YOU COME UP WITH A BETTER ONE?
I WON'T DO WHAT YOU'RE ASKING ME.
COME NOW, DAMIEN! DON'T BE—!
LET HIM BE, HILDE.

THE KID NEVER LISTENS. HE DOES EVERYTHING HE CAN TO GO AGAINST HIS FAMILY.

PERHAPS I WOULDN'T GO AGAINST MY FAMILY IF IT WASN'T FULL OF KILLERS!

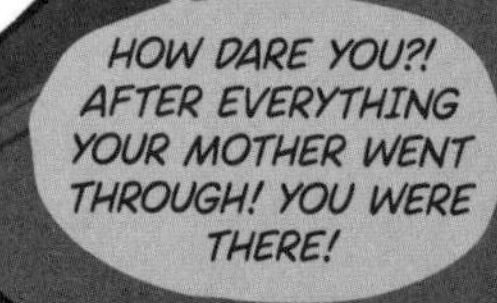
HOW DARE YOU?! AFTER EVERYTHING YOUR MOTHER WENT THROUGH! YOU WERE THERE!

THAT ISN'T AN EXCUSE TO KILL INNOCENTS.
INNOCENTS?! THIS VILLAGE DOESN'T RESPECT US.
LAST WEEK WE WERE VANDALIZED. YOU'VE SEEN WHAT THEY WROTE ON THE HOUSE...

IF I HAD CAUGHT THEM, THEY'D ALREADY BE DEAD.
I'M SURE IT WAS THOSE OLD FRIENDS OF YOURS...

YOU KILLED THEIR PARENTS.
YES. AND NOW YOU'LL DO THE SAME THING TO THEM IF YOU WANT TO SHOW US YOU'RE ON OUR SIDE.
WHAT ARE YOU SAYING?!
YOU'RE THE HEIR OF THE WYTTE FAMILY! SHOW IT FOR ONCE AND DO WHAT YOU MUST!
I DON'T WANT ANYTHING TO DO WITH THIS FAMILY!

OH...

I SHOULDN'T HAVE LEFT THEM.

THAT'S IT, TRAITOR!
GO AWAY AND DON'T COME BACK! I KNEW I SHOULDN'T HAVE TRUSTED YOU!
I'M SORRY, DUDE. BEING A NURSE ISN'T MY THING.
CALL ME WHEN YOU'RE NOT A SWOLLEN BALL OF SNOT.

WHAT'S GOING ON HERE?
WILL IS SICK, POOR THING.
YES, HE'S TRULY UNBEARABLE WHEN HE'S SICK.

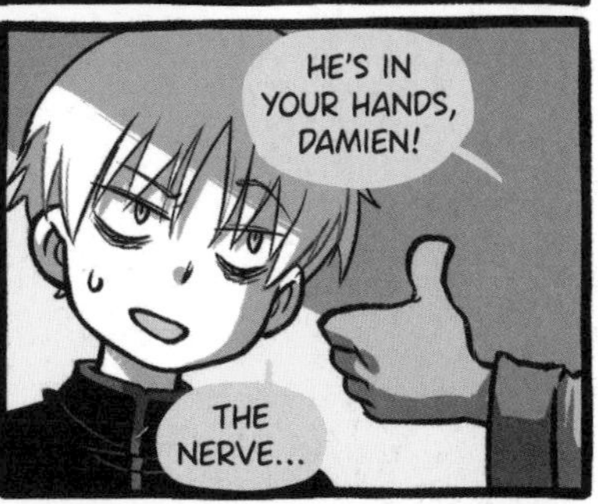
HE'S IN YOUR HANDS, DAMIEN!
THE NERVE...

THAT'S RIGHT, LEAVE ME HERE TO DIE OF DYSENTERY! I HAVE NO DIGNITY LEFT.
HAVE YOU GOT DIARRHEA, WILL? YOU DIDN'T TELL ME!

FORTUNATELY YOU'RE HERE, MONICA!
FULFILLING YOUR DUTY AS MY FUTURE WIFE.

STOP FIDGETING AND LIE BACK.

...
I'M STAYING BECAUSE I WANT TO, NOT BECAUSE IT'S MY DUTY, SILLY!
MY DEAR FRIEND DAMIEN!
YOU'RE ALREADY BACK FROM VISITING YOUR FAMILY? HOW WAS IT?
HORRIBLE.
I'D RATHER TALK ABOUT DIARRHEA.
HA-HA!
HOW LONG HAVE YOU BEEN HERE WITH HIM, MONICA? I CAN STAY IF YOU WANT A BREAK.
DON'T WORRY, I LIKE TO KEEP HIM COMPANY.
BUT YOU'LL GET SICK IF YOU SPEND TOO MUCH TIME IN THIS ROOM.
IT'S FINE! THEN I'LL BE THE ONE WHO GETS TAKEN CARE OF.
WILL YOU STAY THOUGH, DAMIEN? NOW THAT YOU'RE THE KING'S BUTLER, YOU MUST HAVE A LOT TO DO!
SHUT UP AND LAY DOWN.

DAMIEN...

THERE'S SOMETHING...
...I NEED TO TELL YOU.

HUH...?
WHAT IS IT?

I'M AFRAID YOU'LL REJECT ME WHEN I TELL YOU.
WHEN YOU TELL ME WHAT...?

DO YOU KNOW WHY MY FATHER AGREED TO MY MARRIAGE TO MONICA?
BECAUSE HE BETRAYED THE KING.
YES...

MY DAD DID SOMETHING HORRIBLE, DAMIEN.

WHEN I WAS YOUNG, HE GAVE THE ORDER TO BURN A WITCH, EVEN THOUGH BURNING WITCHES WAS FORBIDDEN.
DAMIEN...
BECAUSE OF MY FATHER, YOU ALMOST LOST YOUR MOTHER.
I ALREADY KNOW.
HUH?
I'VE KNOWN FOR A LONG TIME.

CHAPTER 41

COME ON...
TELL ME WHERE THE PRINCE IS...

OKAY, SERIOUSLY, STOP IT.

YOU'RE NOT HELPING BY STANDING THERE AND STARING AT ME.
IT'S NOT OUR FAULT IF YOU AREN'T ANY GOOD AT YOUR OWN MAGIC.
IVY...!
IT'S SO COOL THAT YOU'RE ABLE TO SEE THE FUTURE, NICO.
WE WANT TO WITNESS THIS!

AAAARGH!
WHOAAA!

MARK!
WHAT HAPPENED?
THE TRUCK IS STUCK.

ACTUALLY... WE'RE ALREADY HERE.
WE JUST NEED TO REACH THE CITY.

NO WAY...

THE TRUCK ISN'T MOVING.
ARE YOU SURE YOU'RE ALL PUSHING?!
UGH...
NOT *ALL* OF US, ACTUALLY...

AMIR!! DO SOMETHING!!
I'M A GOOD STRATEGIZER. I'LL SUPERVISE YOU.
LAZY!

AND THAT APPLIES TO YOU TOO, DORIAN!
DORIAN?!
I'M LOOKING FOR A SPELL TO HELP!

BUT YOU TWO...
ARE THE WORST OF ALL!!
NOT ONLY ARE YOU NOT HELPING US, YOU'RE ADDING MORE WEIGHT TO THE TRUCK.
WE'RE NOT THAT HEAVY!

WE'RE LADIES, WE'D GET SUNBURNED.
YEAH, WE'RE AWARE IT'S HOT...
PRINCESS MONICA, YOU SHOULD GET IN, TOO!
DON'T YOU WORRY, ANNE, I'VE GOT MY EMERGENCY PARASOL.

HEY, YOU... SPIRIT...
CAN YOU LEND US A HAND?

IN YOUR DREAMS!
I'VE ALREADY HELPED YOU TOO MANY TIMES AND YOU DIDN'T GIVE ME ANYTHING WORTHY IN EXCHANGE.
...

I GOT IT!
EVERYBODY, GET OUT OF THE WAY!

AWESOME, DORIAN, IT WORKED!
COME ON, CARLO. YOU CAN DO IT!

LOOK, MONICA...
ALL THIS SUN IS GIVING YOU SPOTS LIKE A LEOPARD!

!!

THEY'RE JUST FRECKLES!
AND DANI AND DORIAN...
I CAN'T STAND THE HEAT...
ARE YOU ALL RIGHT, GUYS?
HA-HA, YOU LOOK LIKE TOMATOES!

WE'RE ALMOST THERE!
COME ON, OR ELSE CARLO WILL LEAVE US BEHIND.
HOW FUN.
HURRY UP!
LET'S GO!

ARE THEY GOING TO LET US INTO THE CITY?
OF COURSE, MAN, I'M THE PRINCE.
OH, PRINCE AMIR!

YOU'VE COME TO SAVE US!
SAVE YOU? FROM WHAT?

DON'T YOU KNOW...?

WE'D BETTER GET INSIDE.
COME WITH ME.
AMIR... YOUR CITY IS A BIT GLOOMY.
THIS ISN'T NORMAL...
I HAVE A BAD FEELING, DORIAN...
ME TOO.
SOMETHING BAD HAPPENED HERE.

A DRAGON?!
YES, AMIR...
THE DRAGON HAS BEEN STALKING OUR CITY FOR SOME TIME.
SO THE CRYSTAL BALL WAS RIGHT...
IT HAS EATEN CITIZENS AS WELL AS SOLDIERS WHO HAVE TRIED TO KILL IT.
THIS IS TERRIBLE, MOTHER!
BUT WHAT CAN WE DO?
UGH, THE NERVE!
ARE YOU GOING TO ACT LIKE THIS ISN'T YOUR PROBLEM, BROTHER, AS USUAL?
LONG TIME NO SEE, AISHA!
YOU GOT A HAIRCUT. IT'S CUTE!
SHUT UP! WHERE HAVE YOU BEEN ALL THIS TIME?!
ABOUT YOUR QUESTION, AMIR.
YOU ARE OUR PRINCE.

YOU MUST BE THE ONE TO DEFEAT THE DRAGON.
HIM?
ME?
I WAS GOING TO BE THE ONE TO DEFEAT THE DRAGON, MOTHER!

NO!
I'LL GO.
PRINCE WILLIAM COULD BE TRAPPED BY THAT MONSTER.
I CAME HERE TO SAVE HIM, AND IT'S MY DUTY TO FINISH WHAT I STARTED.

EVEN IF I HAVE TO GO BY MYSELF.

YOU WON'T BE ALONE.

I'LL COME WITH YOU.
WE GOT HERE TOGETHER, AND WE'LL FINISH THIS TOGETHER.

OF COURSE, MONICA.
WE'LL DEFEAT THE VILLAINS TOGETHER!
YES!
DID YOU REALLY THINK WE WOULD DITCH YOU NOW, PRINCESS?
YOU CAN COUNT ON ME.
THANKS. I WASN'T EXPECTING ANY LESS.
I...I'LL TRY TO HELP AS MUCH AS I CAN.
MY MOTHER IS FORCING ME, SO...
IF YOU GET IN TROUBLE, YOU'LL NEED OUR HELP!
HA-HA! GUYS... THANK YOU SO MUCH.
WE'LL SAVE WILL.
AND WHEN YOUR CITY IS SAFE, I'LL NEED YOUR HELP TO GET MY KINGDOM BACK.
CONSIDER IT DONE.

I ALSO WANT A STREET NAMED AFTER ME!
AND A STATUE OF ME STRANGLING THE DRAGON.

HA-HA! THAT'D BE COOL!

COME ON, PRINCESS...

EAT SOMETHING AND REST. YOU CAN LEAVE TOMORROW.

LET ME SEE IF I GOT THIS RIGHT...

WE VOLUNTEERED TO SAVE PRINCE WILLIAM TOMORROW, WHICH MEANS...

WE HAVE 12 HOURS TO MAKE PLANS TO DEFEAT A HUGE, FLYING, FIRE-SPITTING MONSTER?!
IF WE DON'T GO TOMORROW, THE DRAGON COULD ATTACK INNOCENTS IN THE CITY!

PLUS, WE DO HAVE SOME TIME TO PLAN.
DORIAN, WHAT DO WE DO?
I SUGGEST WE IMPROVISE SOMETHING.
AND HOW ON EARTH ARE WE GONNA IMPROVISE KILLING A DRAGON, IDIOT?!
NOW THAT I THINK ABOUT IT... DORIAN, AREN'T YOU ABLE TO TAME DRAGONS?!
NO.
LAST TIME THE DRAGON ONLY OBEYED ME BECAUSE HE THOUGHT I WAS HIS MOTHER.
WHY SHOULD WE EVEN BE PART OF THIS MESS, ANNE?
DANI AND MONICA CAN RIDE BROOMS. THAT MIGHT ALREADY BE AN ADVANTAGE.
CARLO CAN FLY TOO. SOME OF YOU CAN CLIMB ON HIS BACK.
!!

ONE HOUR LATER
WHAT'S GOING ON, NICO? YOU'RE ACTING WEIRD.

I'M SORRY I ACTED LIKE AN IDIOT FOR A LONG TIME. I...
ACTUALLY, YOU'RE MY BEST FRIEND.

THANK YOU FOR EVERYTHING.
WHY ARE YOU SAYING THIS NOW? WAIT!
I'M OFF! I'VE GOT THINGS TO DO!

EVEN IF YOU'RE MEAN AND ANNOYING, I DON'T WANT ANYTHING BAD TO HAPPEN TO YOU.
LEAVE ME ALONE, LOSER.

THANKS FOR BRINGING US HERE.
YOU'RE WELCOME, MAN.

YOU'RE SO NICE AND I HAVE NO IDEA HOW YOU'RE ABLE TO STAND IVY.
HUH? WHERE ARE YOU GOING?

DORIAN...
YEAH?
YOU'RE A NICE FREAK.
I LIKE YOU. YOU'RE ACTUALLY REALLY COOL.

YOU DON'T HAVE TO THANK ME.
NICO...

IS THERE SOMETHING WRONG?
YOU'RE ACTING REALLY WEIRD...

LEAVE ME ALONE, FREAK! BYE!

PRINCESS...
I'M TRULY GLAD I MET YOU.
NICO, WAIT—
YOU'RE INCREDIBLE! I MEAN IT.

THE OTHERS TOLD ME YOU'VE BEEN ACTING STRANGE ALL NIGHT...
WHAT'S WRONG?
NOTHING, I HAVE TO—
COME ON, NICO, YOU CAN TRUST ME!

THE THING IS...
THERE'S A CHANCE WE MIGHT DIE TOMORROW.
I WANTED TO MAKE THINGS RIGHT AND AVOID HAVING UNFINISHED BUSINESS BEFORE RISKING MY LIFE.

DON'T BE SO DRAMATIC! WE'VE BEEN IN DANGER MANY TIMES.
THE OTHER TIMES WE WERE CAUGHT BY SURPRISE!
BUT THIS TIME WE ARE WILLINGLY FACING IT,
AND HOPING NOT JUST TO ESCAPE, BUT TO WIN AGAINST A DRAGON.

WHEN YOU PUT IT THAT WAY...
I'LL DO EVERYTHING IN MY POWER TO WIN, BUT...
I DON'T WANT TO HAVE A HEAVY CONSCIENCE WHEN WE FACE WHATEVER WE FIND IN THE DESERT.
WE'LL SURVIVE.
AND SINCE WE'RE TALKING ABOUT IT...
THERE'S SOMETHING I NEED TO ASK YOU.
SWEAR IT'LL STAY BETWEEN US.
OF COURSE, I LOVE SECRETS!
OKAY, THEN. WELL... YOU ALWAYS SAY YOU'RE A LOVE EXPERT, AND I NEED ADVICE.
A SECRET ROMANCE!? EVEN BETTER!
I STILL HAVE SOMETHING IMPORTANT TO SETTLE...
AND IF EVERYTHING GOES WELL... HOPEFULLY...
I MIGHT HAVE MY FIRST KISS.
WHY DIDN'T YOU ASK MARK?

HE'S YOUR FRIEND, AND—
I CAN'T ASK MY RIVAL!
!!
YOU LIKE DANI!?

YOU'RE JUST REALIZING?! LOVE EXPERT, INDEED!
HOW EXCITING! I'M SO HAPPY FOR YOU.

...THANKS. WHAT ABOUT MY ADVICE?

I HAVE NOTHING TO SAY. I'VE NEVER KISSED WILLIAM.

NOW HURRY UP, BEFORE SHE GOES TO BED!
OKAY!

THANK YOU FOR EVERYTHING, MONICA.
GOOD LUCK!

BLAM

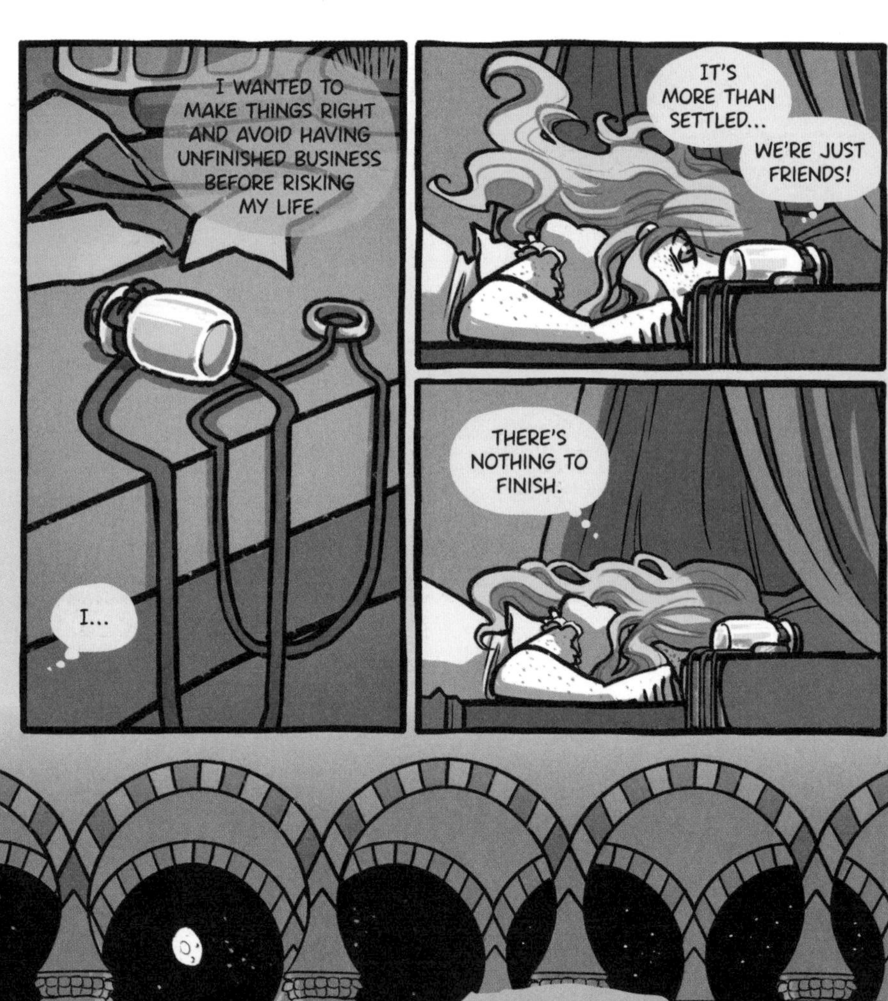
I WANTED TO MAKE THINGS RIGHT AND AVOID HAVING UNFINISHED BUSINESS BEFORE RISKING MY LIFE.
I...
IT'S MORE THAN SETTLED...
WE'RE JUST FRIENDS!
THERE'S NOTHING TO FINISH.

THERE'S NO TIME TO LOSE.
DANI!! THERE'S SOMETHING I NEED TO TELL YOU!

NICO!
YOU SCARED ME! DON'T BURST INTO MY ROOM LIKE THAT!

WHY NOT?
AT THE MASTER'S HOUSE WE SHARED A ROOM, REMEMBER?
YOU SLEPT IN MONICA'S DOLLHOUSE.
IT'S NOT THE SAME.
BAH!

LISTEN, DANI.
I HAVE COMPLETELY IGNORED YOUR PRIVACY BECAUSE I HAVE SOMETHING IMPORTANT TO TELL YOU.

?
WHAT IS IT?
W-WELL—

I DON'T KNOW HOW TO SAY THIS...
YOU SEE...

THIS IS WAY HARDER THAN I THOUGHT!
...
IS IT BAD?
NO! WELL...

IT DEPENDS ON YOU, ACTUALLY...
BUT I DON'T THINK IT'S SOMETHING BAD...

THE TRUTH IS, I...
I REALLY... ARGH!

NICO, COME ON! YOU'RE MAKING ME NERVOUS!

IS THIS A JOKE?

ALLOW ME TO SHOW Y—
I'M DONE WITH THE BATHROOM, DANI!
YOU TOOK FOREVER, DORIAN!

DORIAN, YOU'RE HERE?!
DANI AND I ALWAYS SHARE A ROOM, YOU KNOW THAT.
NICO HAS SOMETHING IMPORTANT TO TELL US!

WHAT'S ALL THIS NOISE?
NOT YOU, TOO!
NICO HAS SOMETHING TO SAY.

WHAT'S GOING ON HERE?
NICO HAS SOME NONSENSE TO TELL US.
YOU'RE UNBEARABLE.
GOOD NIGHT!!
NICO, WAIT...

WHAT DID HE WANT TO TELL US?
NICO'S REALLY WEIRD TODAY...

NICO, HANG ON. WHAT WAS ALL THAT ABOUT?
NONE OF YOUR BUSINESS.
COME OOOON, TELL ME, DUDE.
I'M YOUR BEST FRIEND. DON'T BE MEAN...
YOU'RE ANNOYING.
THE TRUTH IS THAT I DID SEE SOMETHING WEIRD IN THE CRYSTAL BALL.
SOMETHING WEIRD?
I HAVE A FEELING SOMETHING REALLY BAD IS GOING TO HAPPEN.
WHAT... WHAT DID YOU SEE?
IT'S NOT JUST WHAT I SAW...
WHAT DO YOU MEAN?
I SAW DANI CRYING. SHE WAS SURROUNDED BY A DARK AURA...
I GOT THIS FEELING, LIKE SOMETHING'S ABOUT TO CHANGE. SOMETHING'S GOING TO BREAK FOREVER.

CHAPTER 42

IT'S NOT HERE...
WHERE DID I PUT IT?
AAAAGH, IT CAN'T BE!
WHAT'S GOING ON, DORIAN?
I CAN'T FIND MY WAND!
YOU LOST IT?!
I NEVER LOSE STUFF!
DO YOU HAVE YOURS, DANI?
...
OH NO...
I'LL GO—
YES, LET'S GO!
OUCH!
ARE YOU OK?!
POW
THEY LOCKED US IN!
WHAT?!
SPIRIT, PLEASE...
IS THERE SOMETHING YOU CAN DO?
OPEN THE DOOR!

YOU WANT ME TO HELP YOU GET OUT SO THAT YOU CAN FIGHT A DRAGON THAT WILL LIKELY KILL YOU ALL?
YES! PLEASE!
CONSIDER IT DONE.

I NEED A COFFEE...
BOOM
ARGH!

HOW DID YOU DO THAT? DID YOU FIND YOUR WAND?!
THERE'S NO TIME TO EXPLAIN.
LET'S RESCUE THE OTHERS!
?

DON'T WORRY, GIRLS!
WE'RE GONNA GET YOU OUT OF THERE!
STEP AWAY FROM THE DOOR!

BOOM
YOU'RE FREE!
LET'S GO FIND WILLIAM!
HUH? WERE WE TRAPPED? I HADN'T EVEN NOTICED.
ARE WE HAVING BREAKFAST—

NO TIME FOR BREAKFAST.
THERE'S BEEN A BETRAYAL!
SOMEONE IS TRYING TO STOP US FROM DEFEATING THE DRAGON.
I HAVE A FEELING...

I KNOW WHO IT IS.
THIS IS ANNOYING.
NO WAY I'M GOING TO LET AMIR GET ALL THE CREDIT.

BESIDES, THAT NIMROD COULD NEVER DEFEAT THE DRAGON.
AND IT'S NO BUSINESS OF A FOREIGN PRINCESS AND A BUNCH OF BRATS!
IT'S MY DUTY TO PROTECT MY PEOPLE!
I'LL KILL THE DRAGON.
I WONDER IF I'LL BE ABLE TO USE THIS JUNK...
...
AH!

LOOK, OVER THERE.
THAT'S THE DRAGON!
ARE WE IN TIME?
YES, I SEE AISHA!
AISHA!! FASTER, MONICA!
WHAT IS SHE DOING?!
IS SHE GOING TO SHOOT IT?

LOOK, SHE'S GOING TO SHOOT!
THAT WON'T DO ANYTHING BUT ENRAGE IT!
WHA–?
WHAT THE...

HUH?
HOW DARE YOU?
DAMIEN?
WHAT ARE YOU DOING?

GET AWAY FROM HERE, AISHA!
GIVE ME YOUR WAND!
YOU'RE SO ANNOYING!
I WAS ABOUT TO KNOCK DOWN THE DRAGON!
THAT'S EXACTLY WHY! CAN'T YOU SEE WHAT YOU DID TO IT?
IT'S FOR THE SAFETY OF MY PEOPLE!
DON'T YOU GET IT, AISHA?
IF YOU KILL THE DRAGON NOW, IT WON'T TAKE US TO WILLIAM!
DORIAN, WAIT—

DANI, STAY AWAY!
CAN'T YOU SEE THIS ISN'T THE TIME TO FIGHT?!
DORIAN, DON'T BE RIDICULOUS.
REALLY, YOU TWO.
I'M NOT AFRAID OF YOU, DAMIEN!
OR SHOULD I SAY "KING OF WITCHES"?
I THOUGHT YOU WERE SMARTER THAN THIS.
I'M NOT HERE TO HARM ANY OF YOU. I CAME FOR PRINCE WILLIAM.

SERIOUSLY, GUYS, THERE'S A DRAGON BEHIND YOU!
CAN'T YOU LEAVE IT FOR LATER?!
I WON'T LET YOU TAKE PRINCE WILLIAM AGAIN!
WE'RE GONNA SAVE HIM ONCE AND FOR ALL—
DUDE, WHY ARE YOU WEARING BLACK LEATHER IN THE DESERT?
DAMIEN! I'M SO GLAD WE FOUND YOU.
WHERE ARE MY PARENTS?
I BROUGHT THEM WITH ME...
EVERYONE ON THE GROUND!
WATCH OUT!

DAMIEN, COME BACK! TAKE ME WITH YOU!
GIVE ME YOUR BROOM, PRINCESS.
DAMIEN, WAIT!
I HAVE TO FOLLOW IT!
MONICA! ARE YOU OK?!

WHAT JUST HAPPENED?
I HAVE NO IDEA.
YOUR MAJESTY, ALLOW ME TO MAKE INTRODUCTIONS—
!!

MASTER?!

WHAT ARE YOU DOING HERE?
AISHA! WHAT WERE YOU THINKING?
NICO...
YOU'RE ALL SAFE!
I KEPT MY SIDE OF THE BARGAIN WITH DAMIEN.
EVERYTHING'S GOING TO BE ALL RIGHT NOW. WE'RE SAFE.
AH!
KING GEORGE!?
WERE YOU A TOAD JUST NOW?
MONICA, YOUR PARENTS ARE OK!
DAD!
I STILL NEED TO SAVE WILLIAM. WE'RE SO CLOSE...
PLEASE, LET ME GO!
DO WHATEVER YOU NEED TO DO. I TRUST YOU.

CAN I BORROW THIS, DANI?
HUH?
MONICA, NO...!
HOLD ON, WILLIAM!
I'M ALMOST TH—!
ACK!
WHAT'S THE RUSH, PRINCESS?
AREN'T YOU GOING TO WAIT FOR ME?
DORIAN...?

OF COURSE.
LET'S GO!
YES!
LET'S FIND WILL!
THEY LEFT WITHOUT ME! AND TOOK THE BROOMS!
IT'S OKAY, DANI.
NOT TO BE GROSS, BUT...
WE CAN FOLLOW THE TRAIL OF BLOOD.

CHAPTER 43

AISHA, YOU'VE PROVEN YOUR VALUE AND STRENGTH.
BUT TAKE THE WITCHES AND A PAIR OF SOLDIERS.

YOU'LL BE THANKFUL FOR THE COMPANIONSHIP.

BE CAREFUL...

UFFF, HOW LONG UNTIL WE GET THERE?
CAN'T WE STOP TO REST?!
SHUT UP!
IT HASN'T EVEN BEEN TWO HOURS!!
I WAS FORCED TO TAKE YOU WITH ME, AND YOU'RE SLOWING ME DOWN WITH YOUR SNAIL'S PACE!
I DON'T WANT TO HEAR ANY COMPLAINING!!

...
OF COURSE YOU'RE DOING BETTER, YOU'VE GOT A SOLDIER CARRYING A PARASOL FOR YOU!

I'M TALKING TO HIM, TOO! YOU'RE SLOWING ME DOWN!
LEAVE HER ALONE, MAN.
I'M TRULY SORRY PRINCESS, BUT HEAT STROKE IS A VERY REAL DANGER.

THIS ISN'T A RACE, AND WE NEED REST.

NO, NICO.
PRINCESS AISHA IS RIGHT.
WE NEED TO GET THERE AS SOON AS WE CAN TO HELP.
THERE'S NO TIME TO LOSE.
THAT... THAT'S TRUE!
I'M SORRY, I'M JUST REALLY TIRED.
WELL, GATHER ALL YOUR STRENGTH. OUR FRIENDS NEED US!
I STILL DON'T GET WHY AISHA NEEDS TO BE THE GROUP LEADER.
BECAUSE SHE'S THE PRINCESS!
BECAUSE I'M WAY MORE RESOURCEFUL AND PREPARED THAN ALL OF YOU, THAT'S WHY!
YES, YES, THAT'S WHY.
I'M NOT SAYING YOU AREN'T STRONG ENOUGH BUT YOU'RE, WHAT, 10 YEARS OLD?
COME ON, NICO, DON'T BE LIKE THAT.
PRINCESS AISHA IS CLEARLY OLDER THAN YOU.

ACTUALLY, THE PRINCESS JUST CELEBRATED HER 17TH BIRTHDAY.
REALLY? I THOUGHT YOU WERE YOUNGER THAN ME AS WELL, AISHA!
WHAT?! YOU LIAR!!
SEE?
YOU'RE ALL SO RUDE!!
THERE ARE FRESH BLOOD STAINS OVER HERE.
THAT MEANS THE DRAGON IS CLOSE. AND WILLIAM.
OR IT'S A TRAP. MAYBE WE SHOULD TURN AROUND.
WHEN DID YOU BECOME SUCH A COWARD?!
HA-HA, IT WAS A TEST! AND YOU PASSED, DANI!
WHAT THE...?
I'LL SHOW YOU A TEST...

THEY'RE SO NOISY...
IF THIS IS A TRAP, THEY'LL DEFINITELY GET US CAUGHT.
DANI!!
NO!!
HUH?
WHAA?!
WATCH OUT, NICO!

LOOK BEHIND YOU!
AH?!
UGH!
HEY, GIRL!
WE'RE TOO HIGH UP. YOU'RE GOING TO DIE!
OH!
I'M NOT GONNA DIE. I KNOW SOME TRICKS TO AVOID GETTING CRUSHED.

BUT I CAN'T PROTECT EVERYONE BY MYSELF, SPIRIT.
UGH...
PROMISE ME YOU'LL TAKE CARE OF IT!
WHAT...?!
CONSIDER IT DONE!
I'LL PROTECT YOUR FRIENDS.
OH NO.

THE ALARM WENT OFF.
SOMEONE'S GETTING CLOSE TO PRINCE WILLIAM.
WHOEVER IT IS...
THE GUARDIANS WILL ELIMINATE THEM. THE PROTECTION SPELL IS WORKING.
WELL...HILDE, ANGELA, PACK YOUR THINGS.
WE NEED TO GET OUR KING BACK.
WHO ARE THEY?
DAMIEN?
PRINCESS MONICA?
DANI!
ARE YOU OK? CAN YOU HEAR ME?!
LOUD AND CLEAR!
WE'LL TALK LATER, I'M BUSY NOW.
NO, NO, NO! YOU CAN'T FACE THESE VERMIN ON YOUR OWN!

SPIRIT, PROTECT THEM.
AH!
WHAT THE...?
OF COURSE.
WHAT KIND OF SORCERY IS THIS?!
I CAN'T MOVE!
PRINCESS, STOP SHOOTING ARROWS OR WE'LL BE STABBED!
AND NOW...
GET READY, MONSTERS!

DANI'S FINALLY HERE...AND YOU'RE GOING TO EAT HER DUST!

T... THAT'S... TRUE...

UGH...
I THINK THEY'RE MULTIPLYING!
SPIRIT, DO SOMETHING!
DIDN'T YOU SAY YOU'D DO THIS ON YOUR OWN?

LET ME GO, YOU EVIL SNAKE!

SPIRIT, LET MY FRIENDS GO!
FINE...
DANI, HOW DID YOU DO THAT? WHERE'D YOU LEARN THAT SPELL?
THERE'S NO TIME TO EXPLAIN.
RUN, EVERYONE!
EVERYBODY GET IN THE CAVE. HURRY UP!
IT'S TOO HEAVY.
WE WON'T BE ABLE TO CLOSE IT!
BOOM
UGH!

...

ARE YOU GUYS OK?

YEAH...

SOMEONE DO SOMETHING!

DANI, COULD YOU TURN A MAGIC LIGHT ON?

I DON'T KNOW... SPIRIT?

YOU'RE SO ANNOYING.

WHAT ARE YOU SAYING, DANI?

NOTHING.

DID YOU HEAR THAT?

STOP SCARING ME, MARK!

OH, CARLO!

DOES YOUR FROG SPIT FIRE?!

GOOD BOY.
LET THERE BE LIGHT.
HE HE HE HE
OH, WELL DONE, CARLO AND NICO!
WELL, NICO, YOU HAVE GOOD IDEAS SOMETIMES.
WHAT DO YOU MEAN, SOMETIMES...?!
I...I MUST ADMIT YOU'RE IMPRESSING ME, DANI! YOUR MAGIC IS INCREDIBLE.
REALLY? THANK YOU SO MUCH!
PLEASE, TEACH ME HOW TO PERFORM THIS POWERFUL MAGIC.
WH...? ARE YOU SERIOUS? MY BROTHER DORIAN IS THE ONE WHO DOES THAT.
I HAVEN'T SEEN YOUR BROTHER'S MAGIC, BUT ONE THING I KNOW FOR SURE IS THAT YOURS IS GREAT.
I'D BE REALLY GLAD TO HAVE YOU AS A TEACHER, DANI!

OH.

MARK, DUDE, I THINK YOU'RE BLEEDING.
REALLY?

ARE YOU HURT, MARK?
DON'T WORRY, JUST A SCRAPE FROM THE ROCKS.
I DIDN'T EVEN NOTICE IT.

WELL, LET'S MOVE.
WATCH YOUR STEP!
DO YOU THINK THIS CAVE HAS ANOTHER EXIT? WE CAN'T GET OUT THE WAY WE GOT IN.
WELL, GUYS, LOOKS LIKE WE'RE GOING TO GET WET.

THE PATH IS FLOODED.
OH NO...
CAN EVERYONE SWIM?

TO BE HONEST, I DON'T KNOW HOW TO SWIM.
HUH?!

UH... I...

DON'T WORRY, DANI, I'LL CARRY YOU!

THANKS, NICO, BUT MARK IS ALREADY CARRYING ME.
WHAT?!
IT'LL BE EASIER FOR ME.
PLUS, YOU CAN'T LET THE TORCH GO OUT!

OF COURSE NOT.
MARK, AM I TOO HEAVY?
NOT AT ALL. IN WATER YOU'RE EVEN LIGHTER.
LESS TALKING, MORE SWIMMING. WE'RE IN A HURRY!
YOU'RE RIGHT, NICO.
YOU'RE SO FAST, MA—
HUH?
WHY DID YOU STOP? DID YOU PULL A MUSCLE?

CAN YOU HEAR THAT? IT SOUNDS LIKE MUSIC...
MARK...?
HEY, WHERE ARE YOU GOING?!
COME HERE...
DON'T BE AFRAID...
CLOSER...
HURRY...

BE MINE...
WHAT KIND OF MONSTERS ARE THESE? MERMAIDS?
MY ARROWS, QUICK!
WHAT ARE YOU LAUGHING AT, MONSTER?
I'LL WIPE THAT SMILE OFF YOUR FACE!
WAIT!
MARK, DANI!

TAKE THAT!
IT DODGED MY ATTACK.
THEY'RE GETTING AWAY!
...
THEY TOOK THEM...
NOOO!!

CHAPTER 44

MONICA, CAN YOU GET CLOSER TO DAMIEN?
YES, BUT HOLD ON TIGHT!

HEY, DAMIEN!
HOW COOL, OUR FIRST ADVENTURE TOGETHER!
AND THE LAST ONE TOO, I HOPE.
ARE YOU ON OUR SIDE, THEN?

WERE YOU AWARE OF MOM AND DAD'S PLANS?
OF COURSE I WAS. THE FACT THAT YOU BOTH WEREN'T IS RIDICULOUS.

THEN WHY DID YOU LEAVE US BEHIND WHEN YOU RAN AWAY?

WHY DID YOU ABANDON US?

DORIAN, I...
AT THAT TIME...
UGH!
DAMIEN!
CAREFUL, THE DRAGON!

UGH...
WHERE ARE WE?
UH...
THE BROOM'S BROKEN...

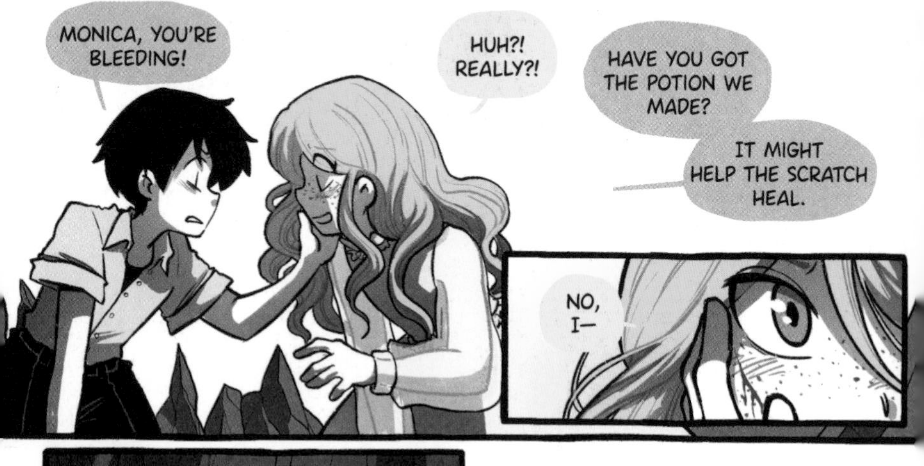
MONICA, YOU'RE BLEEDING!
HUH?! REALLY?!
HAVE YOU GOT THE POTION WE MADE?
IT MIGHT HELP THE SCRATCH HEAL.
NO, I—

THE TRUTH IS, DORIAN...WE'RE NOT SO DIFFERENT, YOU AND I.
YOU DON'T ALWAYS STICK WITH YOUR FAMILY.
DIDN'T YOU JUST LEAVE DANI BEHIND?
THAT'S NOT TRUE! I LEFT HER IN A SAFE PLACE!
WHAT IF YOU DIE FIGHTING, DORIAN?

DOESN'T THAT MEAN ABANDONING THOSE YOU LOVE?
I AM NOT PLANNING TO DIE, PRECISELY BECAUSE OF DANI.
AND THIS MISSION IS TEMPORARY.
IT CAN'T BE COMPARED TO ALL THE YEARS YOU LEFT US AT OUR PARENTS' MERCY.
I KNOW.

YOU RAN AWAY, DAMIEN, YOU CAN'T DENY THAT.
I KNOW THAT, DORIAN.
DO YOU THINK I HAVEN'T ALWAYS KNOWN?
DO YOU THINK I DIDN'T FEEL GUILTY ABOUT THE ONES I LEFT BEHIND?

I JUST WANT US TO WORK TOGETHER.

AT THE END OF THE DAY, WE'RE ON THE SAME SIDE.
ALL RIGHT.

YOU'VE CHANGED.
YOU'RE NOT A CRYBABY ANYMORE.
LET'S DEFEAT THE DRAGON.
AND SAVE WILLIAM.
AND GO BACK TO DANI.

AND THEN...
...WE'LL MAKE MOM AND DAD SEE REASON.
...WE'LL DESTROY OUR PROGENITORS.

I CAN'T BELIEVE YOU STILL THINK THERE'S HOPE FOR THOSE WRETCHES!!
UH...

WHATEVER, WE NEED TO HURRY.

THE SUN IS SETTING.
WILLIAM IS CLOSE, I CAN FEEL IT!

IT LOOKS LIKE THE DRAGON LOST A TON OF BLOOD.
OH, LOOK...
YOU CAN ALREADY SEE THE MOON!
YOU CAN SUMMON THE LIGHT WITH YOUR MAGIC! ISN'T THAT RIGHT, DORIAN?
I MEAN, WHEN THE NIGHT COMES.
OF COURSE, NO PROBLEM!

WHAT WERE YOU DOING LYING ON THE GROUND, DORIAN?
DID YOU FALL?
OH—OF COURSE NOT!
I WAS JUST EXAMINING THE GROUND!
LOOK... THERE'S THE DRAGON.
IS IT DEAD?!
NO, JUST BADLY INJURED...
BUT IT'S RESTING NOW.
THAT'S ITS CAVE. LOOK AT THE GROUND.
SHHH! SHUT YOUR MOUTHS, YOU TWO!
WHAT'S GOING ON, DAMIEN?

OH MY!
AAAARGH!

DON'T SCREAM, PRINCESS, OR IT'S GOING TO FIND US!!
SORRY...

BUT THOSE ARE HUMAN BONES...
WHAT IF THEY BELONG TO PRINCE WILLIAM?

UH...SORRY, SORRY!
I DIDN'T THINK BEFORE I SPOKE.

I'M SURE IT DIDN'T EAT WILL.
OUR PARENTS PROBABLY USED HIM AS BAIT TO CATCH MONICA AND MY TWO NOSY SIBLINGS.
SO HE'S NEARBY, BUT SAFE.
WILL IS HERE. WE JUST NEED TO FIND HIM.

GO, MONICA. FIND WILLIAM.
I'LL KEEP AN EYE ON THE DRAGON.
OKAY...

BUT WHERE SHOULD I START?
THIS IS SUCH A BIG PLACE...

AND I CAN'T FOLLOW THE TRAIL OF RED STAINS ANYMORE...
ALL THE ROSES ARE STRAINED.
TOO BAD, WHITE ROSES ARE SO BEAUTIFUL.

WAIT. WHITE ROSES...
AND ASHES...
THIS REMINDS ME...

I SEE A VERY HIGH TOWER.
FULL MOON NIGHTS, WHITE ROSES, ASHES, AND FIRE. BUT IN OPPOSITE ORDER.
AH...

THE MASTER'S PROPHECY...
PERHAPS...
DORIAN, DAMIEN, KEEP AN EYE ON THE DRAGON.
I'LL BE RIGHT BACK!
BE CAREFUL!!
WHERE ARE YOU GOING?
I THINK I FOUND WILL!
WHAT?
MONICA, WAIT!
MONICA!
DON'T...!

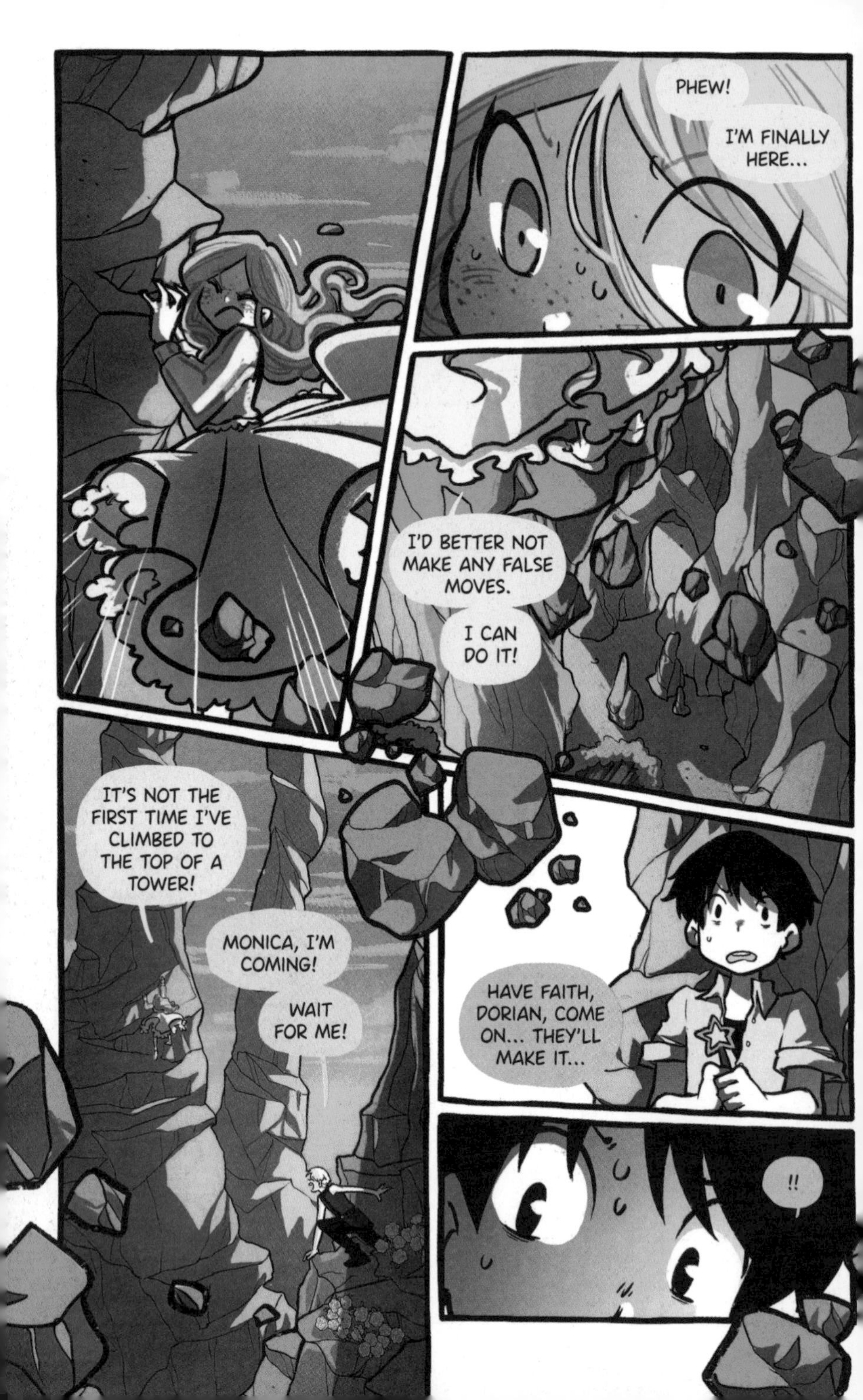
PHEW!
I'M FINALLY HERE...
I'D BETTER NOT MAKE ANY FALSE MOVES.
I CAN DO IT!
IT'S NOT THE FIRST TIME I'VE CLIMBED TO THE TOP OF A TOWER!
MONICA, I'M COMING!
WAIT FOR ME!
HAVE FAITH, DORIAN, COME ON... THEY'LL MAKE IT...
!!

THE DRAGON IS AWAKE?!
NOT FOR LONG!!
DORIAN!
WHAT HAPPENED?
THE DRAGON IS ATTACKING DORIAN!
IT LOOKS LIKE MY BROTHER HAS EVERYTHING UNDER CONTROL FOR...
...NOW?!
HURRY, IT'S SHOOTING FIRE AT US!

THAT'S A GOOD SIGN.
WHAT?!
IT DOESN'T WANT US TO FOLLOW THIS PATH... WILLIAM MUST BE HERE!!
IT'S GETTING CLOSER?!
WHERE'S DORIAN?
RUN, YOU TWO! I CAN'T HOLD OUT MUCH LONGER!!
ARGH!

THE GROUND...
RUN, DAMIEN!!
ARGH!
MONICA!
DAMIEN!!
UGH...

THAT WAS CLOSE.

ARE YOU ALL RIGHT, DAMIEN?
I AM, BUT DORIAN...
HE VANISHED.
HIM AND THE WRETCHED DRAGON.

HUH?! *WHERE DID THAT HOLE COME FROM?!*
DORIAN MUST HAVE FALLEN.
WE NEED TO HELP HIM!!
YES, BUT WE NEED TO FIND WILL FIRST.
MY BROTHER CAN HANDLE HIMSELF. WE DIDN'T COME THIS FAR JUST TO TURN BACK.

BUT, DAMIEN, DORIAN MIGHT BE—
DON'T THINK ABOUT THAT NOW!

THE SOONER WE FIND WILL, THE SOONER WE CAN LOOK FOR DORIAN.

IT'S SO COLD IN HERE...
AH...
THAT'S...
OH!
FINALLY...
...WILLIAM!

CHAPTER 45

STAY WITH US, YOUNG ADVENTURER...
OH MY... HOW GRIM.
FOR AN ETERNITY...
YOU'LL FIND PEACE BY OUR SIDES...
MARK, IT'S ME, DANI!
DON'T LISTEN TO THEM!
MARK!
THERE'S NO WAY...
HE'S COMPLETELY UNDER THEIR SPELL.

AND ON TOP OF THAT, IT SEEMS LIKE THESE MERMAIDS FEED ON HUMAN FLESH...
I BET I'LL BE THEIR DINNER TONIGHT.
BUT WHAT DO THEY WANT FROM MARK?
HE'S HANDSOME, MAYBE THEY JUST LIKE HIM.
I CAN'T JUDGE THE MERMAIDS.
I TRIED TO GIVE HIM A LOVE POTION ONCE, AFTER ALL—
AH!
OF COURSE!
PSST! HEY, MERMAID! OVER HERE!
WHAT?
I SEE THAT YOU CAN SEDUCE PEOPLE WITH YOUR SINGING.
BUT SINGING ALL THE TIME MUST BE TIRESOME, RIGHT?
I'M A WITCH.
LET ME OUT AND I'LL SHOW YOU A POTION THAT WILL BE VERY USEFUL TO YOU...
AAAARGH!

YOU WON'T GET AWAY...WICKED CREATURES.
MARK!!
HEY, THAT'S ENOUGH. GET ME OUT OF HERE.
DANI?
AARGH! HE'S ENCHANTED!
YOU AREN'T GETTING OUT OF HERE ALIVE, MONSTERS!
LET ME GO!
YOU'RE A TRAITOR!
WE HAD A DEAL.
WE SHOULD GO CALL FOR REINFORCEMENTS. WE NEED TO FIND NICO!
AND RESCUE DORIAN, MONICA, DAMIEN, AND PRINCE WILLIAM. REMEMBER?
THAT'S TRUE. NICO IS...! AND DORIAN, AND MONICA!
I'LL GET YOU OUT OF THERE RIGHT AWAY. WE NEED TO HURRY!
YESSS!!
ARGH!

UH-OH.
WHAT THE...?
RUN!
YOU'RE NOT RUNNING AWAY!! YOU HEAR ME?
HELP ME OR THIS THING IS GONNA EAT ME!!
WE'LL JUST HAVE TO USE THESE STONES.
PRINCESS! ARE YOU KIDDING?!
HELP ME! WE CAN'T LEAVE HIM HERE TO BE THE MONSTER'S DINNER.
THAT WAS MY LAST ARROW!
I DON'T KNOW, JUST DO SOMETHING!
IT WORKED! HE'S FREE!
WE DID IT!

UH... IT DOESN'T LOOK...VERY HAPPY.
NO, IT DO—
RUN!
RUN WHILE YOU CAN!
WHERE CAN I GO?!
HEY, DON'T LEAVE ME HERE!
WE ALREADY FREED YOU!
ARGH, CARLO! DON'T BITE ME!
WHAT'S WRONG WITH YOU?
OH, YOU FOUND A WAY OUT...
BUT YOUR BUTT BARELY FITS! I'M AFRAID I WON'T FIT EITHER.

ARGH!
THAT WAS CLOSE...
CARLO! WHERE DID YOU COME FROM?
HUH?
IT'S...
DANI? IS THAT YOU?!
NICO?!
I'M SO GLAD YOU'RE SAFE! WHERE'S MARK?
HE'S WITH ME. HOW DID YOU GET DOWN THERE?
IT'S A LONG STORY...
MOVE, I'LL TRY TO TEAR DOWN THE WALL.
NO, NO, IF YOU TEAR DOWN THAT WALL—
UGH!!
NICO?!

CAN YOU GET OUT OF THERE?!
THE MONSTER IS BLOCKING THE EXIT!
IF YOU TEAR DOWN THE WALL, THIS MONSTER WILL CHASE US.
PUT A SPELL ON ME. MAKE ME SMALL AGAIN! I'LL BE ABLE TO PASS THROUGH.
ARGH!!
WHAT... A-ARE YOU SURE, NICO?
YES! YOU'LL GET ME BACK TO MY ORIGINAL SIZE, NO PROBLEM. JUST HURRY!
OKAY!

ARE YOU...?!

I'VE GOT YOU!
YOU MEAN *I'VE* GOT *YOU*.
DEAREST DANI, YOU SAVED MY LIFE.
THAT WAS CLOSE.
THE MONSTER LOOKS ANGRY.
OH, NICO, YOU'RE SO CUTE.
IT'S TRUE, I DIDN'T REMEMBER HOW CUTE YOU LOOKED IN MINI!
YEAH, RIGHT. NOW GET ME BACK TO MY ORIGINAL SIZE.
I DON'T KNOW HOW. WE NEED DORIAN.
UGH, FINE. I'M A NEW MAN, I CAN HANDLE IT.
LOOK! THE SKY...! WE MIGHT HAVE FOUND AN EXIT.
REALLY?

RIGHT THERE.
WE'RE COMING, DORIAN!
REINFORCEMENTS ARE ON THE WA—
EH?!
WHAT'S THAT?
WITCHES ON BROOMSTICKS?
THAT CAN'T BE...!
WE HAVE TO FOLLOW THEM. I'M SURE THEY'LL TAKE US TO DORIAN AND THE OTHERS.
YES, AND WE'LL KICK THEIR BUTTS ONCE AND FOR ALL.
THERE ARE TOO MANY...
BUT WE'VE GOT YOU, DANI. YOU'RE INVINCIBLE!
NO WAY. MY POWERS—
YOUR POWERS WHAT? YOU JUST SAVED US!
WELL SAID!

YOUR WEIRD SPELLS SAVED OUR LIVES.
MAYBE YOU GUYS ARE RIGHT.
OF COURSE WE ARE!
YOU'RE A VERY POWERFUL WITCH, DANI.
PERHAPS IN THE END...
I'LL BE ABLE TO LEARN FROM MY MISTAKES.
I CAN BECOME A STRONG PERSON, LIKE DORIAN...

CHAPTER 46

WILL! I'M SO GLAD YOU'RE OKAY!!
I ALMOST BELIEVED YOU WERE DEAD.

...
I SAW YOU ON THE FLOATING ROCK, BUT I COULDN'T TALK TO YOU. WILL...
CAN YOU HEAR ME? WHY AREN'T YOU WAKING UP?

I HAVE AN IDEA! THIS HEALING POTION—

AH... EMPTY. RIGHT.

PRINCESS, HE'S NOT GOING TO WAKE UP.
OF COURSE HE IS! I CAN HEAR HIS HEARTBEAT, DAMIEN. COME LISTEN.
I KNOW HE'S ALIVE. BUT HE'LL ONLY WAKE UP FOR...

TRUE LOVE'S KISS.
SERIOUSLY? LIKE IN A FAIRY TALE?!
I'M AFRAID SO... MY MOTHER HAS A SILLY SENSE OF HUMOR.
WHAT ARE YOU TALKING ABOUT? IT'S SO ROMANTIC!
AFTER SO MANY DANGERS, THE PROPHECIES OF A WITCH, FIGHTING A DRAGON, AND KISSING A SLEEPING PRINCE,
PRINCESS MONICA WILL GO BACK TO THE PALACE ALONG WITH HER FRESHLY RESCUED FIANCÉ, RIDING A WHITE HORSE.
THEY'LL WRITE SONGS ABOUT MY BRAVERY!
I THINK I'M GOING TO BE SICK...
FINALLY, WILL...

I'M JUST ONE KISS AWAY FROM SAVING YOU ONCE AND FOR ALL.
AND AFTER THAT, WE'LL BE TOGETHER...
JUST ONE KISS AWAY...
I CAN'T DO IT.
...A TRUE LOVE'S KISS.

WHAT DO YOU MEAN?
GO ON, KISS HIM!
I DON'T DARE, DAMIEN.

WHAT IF HE DOESN'T WAKE UP?
I ALREADY TOLD YOU, I'M ALMOST SURE THIS IS HOW THE CURSE WORKS.
THIS IS THE PERFECT BAIT FOR YOU.
WHAT IF MY KISS DOESN'T WAKE HIM UP?
IT HAS TO BE TRUE LOVE...
WHAT IF I DON'T ACTUALLY...?
AFTER ALL OF THIS...?

WHY ARE YOU WORRYING ABOUT THIS NOW?
OF COURSE IT'LL WAKE HIM UP.
HOW CAN YOU BE SO SURE?

BECAUSE. I KNOW YOU LOVE HIM.

BUT WHAT IF...

WHAT IF I LOVE ANOTHER PERSON MORE?
I'M A HORRIBLE PERSON, AREN'T I?
I BETRAYED HIM, AND NOW HE'LL NEVER WAKE UP.

OF COURSE YOU'RE NOT HORRIBLE.
JUST BECAUSE YOU LOVE OTHER PEOPLE?
WE ALL LOVE MANY PEOPLE IN DIFFERENT WAYS.

THAT DOESN'T CHANGE YOUR LOVE FOR WILL.
IF IT WOULD MAKE YOU FEEL BETTER, I COULD DO IT.

...WHAT? YOU?
WELL, I'M NOT ACTUALLY DYING TO KISS WILL WHILE HE'S ASLEEP.
BUT I HAVE NO DOUBT HE'LL WAKE UP IF I DO.
DAMIEN, DO YOU—?
WHAT WAS THAT?
WE'VE GOT COMPANY.
BOOM
WHOA!
OH MY, WE'RE INTERRUPTING SOMETHING.
WE FINALLY CAUGHT YOU, PRINCESS.
AND DAMIEN, YOU'LL BE SORRY TO HAVE DISAPPOINTED YOUR FATHER.

I KNEW WE SHOULDN'T HAVE LISTENED TO THAT STUPID PROPHECY—
I WON'T LET YOU HURT HIM!
HE'S YOUR SON! HOW COULD YOU?
OH, LITTLE PRINCESS. HOW WOULD YOU STOP THIS?
WE WILL STOP THIS.
IT LOOKS LIKE THEY'RE STRUGGLING IN THERE, MRS. WYTTE.
SHOULD WE GO HELP THEM?

NOBODY MAKES A MOVE UNLESS I SAY SO.
WE NEED TO STAY VIGILANT. DAMIEN AND THE FORMER KING WON'T MAKE IT EASY FOR US.
AH...
IT'S BREAKING...
?
COULD IT BE...?
COME ON, DAMIEN! ATTACK!!
WATCH OUT!
WE'LL TURN YOU INTO A TADPOLE, PRINCESS!
AAAARGH!!
NO!

I MISSED!
HUH...?
DON'T WORRY ABOUT ME, I'LL FIND A WAY TO ESCAPE!
LET ME GO!
YOU DON'T STAND A CHANCE, PRINCESS!
DAMIEN, GET WILL OUT OF HERE!
WILL IS STILL UNDER THE CURSE.
...
OH, COME ON!

DAMIEN...?
OH, DAMIEN, I'M SO GLAD TO SEE YOU!
WHERE ARE WE—?
THERE'S NO TIME TO EXPLAIN!

YOUR FIANCÉE IS IN DANGER!
DAMIEN, WHAT DID YOU JUST—
POW
WILL! YOU'RE FINALLY AWAKE!

MONICA!!
DON'T WORRY! YOUR PRINCE WILLIAM IS HERE TO RESCUE YOU!
WILL, YOU'RE UNARMED—!

BOOM
NOW WHAT?
DRAGONS!

COME ON, DANI, IT'S 7:30, TIME TO GET—
UGH!
WHAT THE...?
SLIMY. AND IT SMELLS LIKE ASHES...
CARLO?
OH.
OH.
OH...
LITTLE DRAGOOON!!
YOU'RE HUGE!!
I MISSED YOU!
WHAT DID YOU SAY?
I GREW UP TOO?

SO TELL ME, WHAT HAVE YOU BEEN UP TO LATELY?
MONITORING?
MONITORING WHAT...?
UH...
OH.
WE HAVE TO GET OUT OF HERE.

ALMOST THERE...
MONICA MIGHT BE IN DANGER...
YOU CAN DO IT, DORIAN.
JUST A LITTLE BIT MORE...
HUH?!
ARGH!!
POW
OUCH!!
POW
POW
UGH...

CAN'T YOU HELP ME OUT HERE?!
HEY, LISTEN!!
OOPS!
I SHOULD STOP SCREAMING, OR I'LL WAKE UP YOUR BROTHERS.
COME ON, HELP ME OUT... QUIETLY.
BOOM
WHAT'S GOING ON OUT THERE?
WE'RE CLOSE, I CAN HEAR THE EXPLOSIONS.
YES, WE CAN ALL HEAR IT!
WHAT IS IT?
BOOM
BOOM

BOOM
THERE THEY ARE.
HURRY UP, DRAGON.
GET READY TO FLY!
THEY WON'T KNOW WHAT HIT THEM.
EH?!

DRAGONS...
ALL OF THE DRAGONS.
ARE THEY HUGE OR HAVE I SHRUNK TOO MUCH?
NO...
THEY'RE HUMONGOUS!!
THE DRAGONS ARE OUT OF CONTROL!
AGAIN?!
OH NO...
THERE'S... DORIAN?!

OW...
I'M IN CONTROL.
I CAN DO IT!
ISN'T THAT MR. WYTTE'S YOUNGEST SON?
HE'S A DRAGON RIDER!
WHY DID THEY CHOOSE THAT TRAITOR DAMIEN AS OUR KING...?
THIS GUY SEEMS WAY MORE POWERFUL!
WHAT?!

OH.

WE NEED A DRAGON RIDER!
DOES ANYONE KNOW HOW TO TAME THEM?

IT LOOKS LIKE THEY FOUND PRINCE WILLIAM...

DAMIEN CAN'T RULE US ANYMORE. THAT MUCH IS CLEAR.
THAT'S WHY I'LL BE THE NEW KING. DAMIEN WILL END UP IN A DUNGEON!
BUT, HANS... THE PROPHECY SAID THE KING HAD TO BE A CHILD. AND DORIAN SEEMS LIKE THE RIGHT CHOICE.

YOU MUST BE JOKING, HILDE!
AH, MR. WYTTE... I THINK WE HAVE A PROBLEM...!

SHUT UP!

THERE YOU GO, MONICA!
YOU CAN FLY, CAN'T YOU?
YES, OF COURSE!
LET'S GO KILL THE DRAGON, DAMIEN!
WE'RE GETTING OUT OF HERE RIGHT NOW.

MONICA...

WE'VE ALMOST MADE IT.
SOON ENOUGH WE'LL BE BACK HOME.

SOON!

COME BACK HERE, DAMIEN!
THROW SOME FREEZER SPELLS AT THEM!

AH!

WATCH OUT!
THAT'S DORIAN'S DRAGON!
HE'S NOT CONTROLLING IT?!
THE DRAGON'S CONVINCED THAT DORIAN IS ITS MOTHER.
IT WON'T HARM HIM, BUT THAT DOESN'T MEAN IT WILL OBEY EVERYTHING HE SAYS.
THE DRAGON'S GOING THROUGH PUBERTY, AFTER ALL!!
DAMIEN AND WILLIAM?!
CALM DOWN, DRAGON!
YOU DO NOT ATTACK OUR FRIENDS!
STOP IT!
NO...

WHERE ARE THEY?
LOOK, THE YOUNG WYTTE BRUSHED OFF HIS RIVALS TO THE THRONE.
HE JUST ATTACKED HIS BROTHER!
AND MR. WYTTE TOO.
HE KILLED PRINCE WILLIAM!
NO...
THAT'S...
HE'S THE NEW KING!
LONG LIVE DORIAN WYTTE, THE KING OF WITCHES!

WILL?
MY DEAR WILLIAM...
PLEASE...
SNIFF...
NO, WILL...!
HUH?!
WATCH OUT, MONICA!
WHAT ARE YOU DOING, DORIAN?!
UGH...I'M SO HOT.
WHAT HAPPENED...?
DORIAN CAN'T CONTROL HIS DRAGON.

STOP! PLEASE, ENOUGH IS ENOUGH.
WILL, YOU'RE OKAY!
OF COURSE.
HANS!
OH NO... MR. WYTTE...
ANSWER ME!
HANS, DON'T DO THIS TO ME!!
YOU CAN'T BE...
DON'T LEAVE ME ALONE WITH THIS MESS, PLEASE!

THEY KILLED MR. WYTTE!
HANS!
NO...
YOU KILLED YOUR FATHER—
STOP.
LOOK, THE DRAGONS ARE CALM.
MAYBE MRS. WYTTE WAS CONTROLLING THEM ALL ALONG.
BUT NOW IT'S TOO LATE...

HIS OWN SON KILLED HIM TO GET THE THRONE!
MOM...
I'M SORRY...
UGH!
THE WYTTES ARE OUT OF CONTROL.
TRAITORS! THE WYTTES ARE MORE POWERFUL THAN ANY OF YOU.

OBEY YOUR NEW KING!
AH...
NICO...
WHY AM I BACK TO NORMAL?
THE SPELL WAS SUPPOSED TO SAVE YOU...
SO WE MUST BE SAFE NOW.

I SHOULD FEEL RELIEVED.

DAD WAS A KILLER.

SO WHY ARE MY HANDS STILL SHAKING?

THE DRAGON'S CHASING US.
DON'T ATTACK, IT WON'T HURT ME!
IT'S RIGHT BEHIND MONICA!
WHAT...?
IT JUST WANTS TO BE BY MY SIDE!
BUT IT'S THE SAME DRAGON THAT KILLED—
GET OUT OF HERE, DRAGON!
DON'T FOLLOW ME AROUND!!

AND DON'T GO BACK TO MY MOTHER!
DON'T LET HER CONTROL YOU!
DON'T LET ME CONTROL YOU!
YOU'RE A DRAGON! *DON'T LET ANYBODY CONTROL YOU!!*
OH...IT UNDERSTOOD...
DORIAN... ARE YOU...?
LET'S GO BEFORE IT CHANGES ITS MIND.
I'M SURE DANI IS WAITING FOR US AT THE PALACE...

OH, THIS IS WHERE AMIR LIVES!
HAVE YOU REALLY JUST REALIZED WHERE WE ARE?
WHERE IS HE?
PROBABLY TAKING IT EASY AS USUAL.
REALLY?! AT LEAST YOU CAME TO RESCUE ME INSTEAD, DAMIEN! AND MONICA!
WE DIDN'T HAVE TIME FOR A PROPER REUNION. COME ON, GIVE ME A HUG!
NOW'S NOT THE TIME.
AND OUR MISSION WAS TO KILL THE DRAGON.
WHAT ARE WE GOING TO TELL AMIR AND HIS MOM?
OH...
HUH?
DORIAN...!
I THOUGHT WE COULD FIX THIS.
I THOUGHT DAD WOULD SEE REASON!
HE ALWAYS KNOWS WHAT'S RIGHT...

WITH TIME... BUT I...
FOR A MOMENT I THOUGHT IT WAS MY MOTHER'S PLAN, BUT...
I WAS RESPONSIBLE! THE WAY SHE LOOKED AT ME! SHE HATES ME—
IT WAS ME ALONE!
UGH.
WE'D BETTER HURRY. WE NEED TO REPORT WHAT HAPPENED.
IT MIGHT BE NECESSARY TO EVACUATE THE CITY.
SHOULDN'T YOU SAY SOMETHING TO YOUR BROTHER? HE'S DEVASTATED.

WHAT DO YOU WANT ME TO SAY?
I DON'T KNOW, BUT HE NEEDS THE SUPPORT OF HIS FAMILY.
DANIELA'S INSIDE THE CASTLE.
SHE'LL GIVE HIM ALL THE SUPPORT HE NEEDS.
AND MONICA'S BY HIS SIDE FOR NOW.
I WOULDN'T FIT THERE.
BUT, DAMIEN...HE WAS YOUR FATHER AS WELL.
HA-HA, I'M AWARE.
OF COURSE IT BOTHERS ME TO WONDER WHAT HE COULD HAVE BEEN...
A FUTURE WHERE MY FATHER COULD SEE REASON, IN DORIAN'S WORDS.
BUT LET'S BE HONEST: THAT WAS NEVER GOING TO HAPPEN.
BESIDES, WILL...
RIGHT NOW I'M TOO HAPPY TO HAVE YOU BACK AND KNOW THAT YOU'RE SAFE.
THEN WHY ARE YOU CRYING?
I HONESTLY DON'T KNOW.

IT'S TRUE. FROM NOW ON EVERYTHING WILL BE OK. I'M HAPPY... RIGHT?
LET US PASS.
JUST THE FOUR OF YOU?
WHAT ABOUT THE PRINCESS?
I'M HERE.
SHE'S HERE.
I MEAN *MY* PRINCESS.
PRINCESS AISHA.
SHE LEFT WITH A COUPLE OF SOLDIERS, TWO BOYS, A WITCH, AND A FLYING TOAD.
WHERE ARE THEY?
THAT CAN'T BE...
DANI'S STILL OUT THERE...?!

I HAVE TO—
DORIAN, WAIT!
WE'LL ALL GO.
I WON'T PUT ANYONE ELSE IN DANGER!
I'LL FIND DANI.
NOT NOW, DORIAN...
COME ON, FLY...!
DON'T FOLLOW ME!!
UGH!!
THAT'S WHAT YOU GET FOR BEING SO STUBBORN!!
WE'RE ALL GOING TO LOOK FOR DANI!!
NOT SO FAST. NO ONE'S GOING ANYWHERE.
HUH?

WE'RE BACK.
AND WE BRING GOOD NEWS.
BUT WHERE'S DANI?

I'M SO GLAD YOU'RE SAFE, PRINCESS—

AISHA!!
IT'S BEEN SO LONG!!

YOU WERE LOOKING FOR ME!
HA-HA, MORE OR LESS.

WE OVERCAME MANY LETHAL CHALLENGES AND ENTERED THE CAVE ONLY TO FIND...

THE DRAGON WAS DEAD, BURIED UNDER A PILE OF ROCKS!

WOW, THAT'S INCREDIBLE, PRINCESS AISHA!
YOU SAVED THE TOWN!
NOT AT ALL! THE DRAGON WAS DEAD WHEN I ARRIVED.
THESE GUYS ARE OUR HEROES!
AISHA... THAT'S NICE BUT...
WHERE'S DANI?!
IT SEEMS LIKE EVERYONE HAS LEFT.
DANI...
COME ON...
WE SHOULD GET GOING, TOO.

OKAY...
HOORAY, WE'RE FREE!
THE DRAGON'S DEAD!
FINALLY! WE'RE SAFE!
I HEARD THE WITCHES DID IT. THE WITCHES SAVED US!
WE'LL FINALLY SLEEP PEACEFULLY.

RIGHT...I HAD FORGOTTEN WE WENT THERE TO KILL A DRAGON.
THE DRAGON IS DEAD, THE PRINCE IS SAFE.
IS THIS SUPPOSED TO BE A HAPPY ENDING, THEN?
YEAH, I THINK SO.
BUT...IT DOESN'T FEEL LIKE A HAPPY ENDING.

WE GOT RID OF THE BEAST THANKS TO MY DAUGHTER, PRINCESS AISHA, ALONG WITH THESE TWO SOLDIERS.
AND OF COURSE, PRINCESS MONICA AND HER GROUP OF WITCHES.

YOU'RE SO THIN, DUDE!
LEAVE ME ALONE, AMIR! YOU DIDN'T EVEN BOTHER TO COME AND RESCUE ME!
OF COURSE I'M THIN, I'VE BEEN ASLEEP FOR MONTHS!

ASLEEP? AND SOMEONE WOKE YOU UP WITH A KISS?
WELL, NOW THAT YOU MENTION IT...

THANKS TO THESE HEROES...

TODAY WE CAN REST PEACEFULLY OR CELEBRATE JOYFULLY.

CHAPTER 49

WILLIAM, THE NIGHTMARE IS OVER.

I'M HAPPY TO SEE THAT YOU'VE STILL GOT YOUR SENSE OF HUMOR.

THANK YOU, SIR.

I ALREADY SENT SOMEONE TO TELL YOUR FATHER.

WE'LL MEET WITH HIM AND FIGURE OUT HOW TO TAKE BACK MY CASTLE...

DORIAN, WHERE ARE YOU GOING?

AND THEN WE'LL CELEBRATE YOUR MARRIAGE TO MY DAUGHTER.

WHAT?! I'M ONLY 14!!

YOU'RE 15, MONICA. YOUR BIRTHDAY WAS A MONTH AGO.

HAPPY BELATED BIRTHDAY, MONICA!

THANK YOU...
BUT THAT'S NOT THE POINT!!
WHY DO I HAVE TO MARRY WILL NOW?!

IF ANYTHING HAPPENS TO ME, THERE'S NO WAY TO KNOW IF WILL'S FATHER WILL REMAIN PEACEFUL.
WE'LL THROW A WONDERFUL PARTY.

WE'LL HELP YOU FIND THE DRESS!
MONICA SEEMS TO LOVE THIS IDEA.

WE NEED TO UNITE THE FAMILIES AS SOON AS POSSIBLE. IF I DIE, YOU'LL BE KING AND QUEEN.
BUT...DAD...
MONICA...

IT ALMOST SEEMS LIKE YOU DON'T WANT TO MARRY ME.

DANI?

WHERE ARE YOU GOING, DORIAN?

WAS SHE...?
DORIAN!

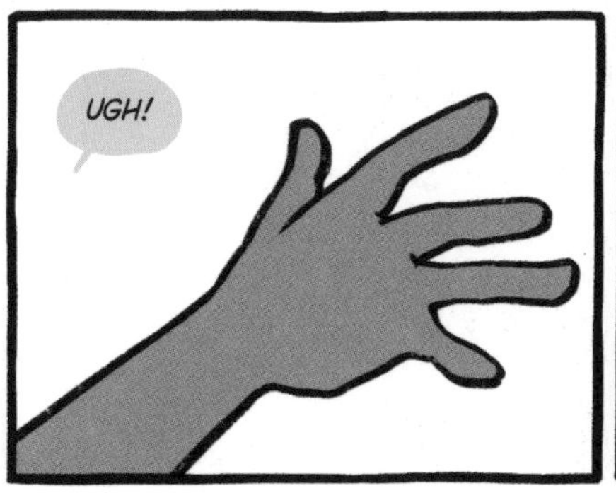
UGH!

DANI!

DANI, I...
I'M NOT SURE IF YOU KNOW WHAT I DID... I—

YOU DID WHAT YOU COULD, DORIAN.
I DID ABSOLUTELY NOTHING.
WHAT ARE YOU TALKING ABOUT?

HEY, LOOK AT ME...
IT DOESN'T MATTER.
EVERYTHING IS ALL RIGHT NOW, DORIAN.
NO. WHAT ARE YOU SAYING?
IT'S ALL WRONG.

I NEED TO THANK YOU.

MY ENEMIES HAVE NO POWER OVER ME NOW.
MY DAUGHTER IS BACK. PRINCE WILLIAM IS BACK.
DANI!
AND THERE'S SOMETHING I LEARNED FROM THIS:

THE WITCHES ARE NOT THE ENEMY.

MAGIC HAS HELPED ME ON MULTIPLE OCCASIONS.

THIS WAR HAS BEEN GOING ON FOR FAR TOO LONG.

NO ONE ELSE WILL DIE OVER MAGIC.

WE'RE NOT AFRAID OF MAGIC ANYMORE, KIDS.

AND IT'S ALL THANKS TO YOU.

THANK YOU, YOUR MAJESTY.

I DON'T KNOW WHAT TO WEAR...
I'M GONNA TAKE A BATH.
NO, I WANNA GO FIRST!
AND WHY IS THAT?
IT TAKES YOU FOREVER TO GET DRESSED!
AND NOW THAT PRINCE WILLIAM'S AROUND, I'M SURE IT'LL TAKE YOU TWICE AS LONG TO DRESS UP!
YOU HAVEN'T EVEN CHOSEN YOUR OUTFIT YET!

BUT I'M ALMOST DONE!
...OKAY.
WHAT?
THIS IS SO HORRIBLE.
I'VE NEVER FELT THIS WAY. IT'S TEARING ME UP INSIDE.
FOR JUST A SECOND, I'D LIKE TO STOP FEELING ANYTHING.

DON'T EVER SAY THAT.
WHAT THE KING SAID... I HOPE MOM WILL SEE REASON.

I'M SURE MOM HATES ME. AFTER WHAT I DID...

WHAT?!
OF COURSE NOT!
AND WHY NOT?

BECAUSE YOU NEVER DID ANYTHING WRONG.
NEVER.
YOU'RE THE ONLY ONE OF US WHO NEVER DID ANYTHING HORRIBLE. AND...

...
AND I LOVE YOU SO MUCH.

...I LOVE YOU TOO, SILLY.
YOU'D BETTER!
I HOPE MOM SEES REASON, TOO.

YEAH...
WELL, I...
I'M GONNA TAKE A BATH!

HEY, DANI, DORIAN!
DO YOU WANT A PIECE OF CAKE?
!!
IT'S ALMOST AS TASTY AS THE ONES MY FATHER BAKES!
DANI...? WHAT ARE YOU WEARING?
THANKS, MARK, BUT I DON'T FANCY ANYTHING SWEET.

THAT DRESS DOESN'T SUIT YOU!
WHAT THE HECK? WE AGREED THAT WE'D TRY TO CHEER HER UP!

SHUT UP, YOU DON'T GET IT!

WHAT ARE YOU—
REMEMBER THE VISION I TOLD YOU ABOUT, WHERE I SAW DANI CRYING INCONSOLABLY?
SHE WAS WEARING THAT DRESS.

I'VE ALREADY GOT SOME IDEAS FOR YOUR WEDDING DRESS, PRINCESS!
YOU'RE SO DILIGENT, ANNE! WELL, I'VE ALSO GOT SOME IDEAS FOR MY BRIDESMAID'S DRESS!
WE NEED TO THROW ONE HELL OF A PARTY—YOU ONLY GET MARRIED ONCE!
WILLIAM AS A MARRIED MAN... HOW SURREAL...
AFTER KNOWING THEM SO LONG, IT DOES FEEL STRANGE.
THEY'VE BEEN ENGAGED SINCE CHILDHOOD.

REALLY? DO YOU HAVE A RING, TOO, WILL?
HEY, EVERYONE...

I THINK NOW ISN'T THE TIME TO CELEBRATE ANYTHING, NOT EVEN VICTORIES OR JOYFUL EVENTS.
I KNOW SOME OF YOU HAVE NO IDEA ABOUT THIS, BUT SOMETHING HORRIBLE HAPPENED TODAY,
SO PLEASE SHOW SOME RESP—

OF COURSE I HAVE THE RING!
IT GAVE ME STRENGTH DURING THE WORST MOMENTS OF MY CAPTIVITY,

WHEN THE WITCHES LOCKED ME UP ON THE FLOATING ROCK.

MONICA ALWAYS WEARS IT TOO, SEE—

AH... WHAT'S THAT?
AN EMPTY FLASK?

WHAT'S THAT PIECE OF GARBAGE DOING AROUND YOUR NECK, MONICA?
GIVE IT BACK! IT'S NOT GARBAGE!
AND WHERE'S THE RING?

IT'S IN MY ROOM!!
NOW WILL YOU PLEASE DROP THE SUBJECT?!

YOU SHOULD WEAR THE RING.

YOU'RE ENGAGED...

PLEASE, DROP IT!!
I DON'T WANT TO MARRY WILL!
WHOA...
I'M SORRY.
WAIT, MONICA!
GOSH...
HA-HA!
YOU GOT SUPER REJECTED, WILLIAM.
POOR THING...
IT MUST BE BECAUSE YOU'RE SKIN AND BONES!
HE'S SHOCKED.
I THOUGHT HER ONLY DREAM IN LIFE WAS TO MARRY HER BELOVED PRINCE!
HOW ODD...
WHY IS SHE ACTING LIKE THIS?
I...
I HONESTLY HAVE NO IDEA.

CHAPTER 50

I'LL TALK TO HER LATER, I'M SURE SHE'LL SEE REASON.

UHM...

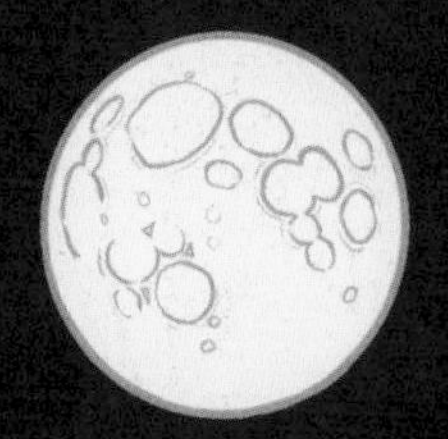

WHAT TIME IS IT?

DORIAN...?

WHERE IS HE?

SPIRIT!

YOUR BROTHER WENT OUT AND I KNOW WHERE HE IS.

THERE'S SOMETHING YOU NEED TO SEE.

WHAT SHOULD I DO NOW?
I CAN'T GO BACK TO MY ROOM. I'M SURE WILLIAM IS WAITING FOR ME THERE.
OR WORSE, MY FATHER.
EVEN THOUGH I SHOULD PROBABLY TALK TO HIM... I NEED TO LET HIM KNOW THAT MY DECISION IS FIRM.

HEY, MONICA...
DORIAN!
IT'S VERY LATE. YOU SHOULD BE ASLEEP!
THE SAME APPLIES TO YOU.
COME ON, DON'T BE SUCH A PAIN IN THE NECK!
I JUST NEEDED SOME FRESH AIR...
MONICA.

THANK YOU FOR SPEAKING UP FOR DANI AND ME TODAY.
YOU'RE THE ONLY ONE WHO DID THAT.
PLEASE, DON'T THANK ME, DORIAN—

BUT I DON'T UNDERSTAND WHY YOU SAID THAT TO PRINCE WILLIAM.

WHY DON'T YOU WANT TO MARRY HIM ANYMORE?
...

CAN'T YOU UNDERSTAND?
NO.
THEN, WHAT ARE YOU DOING HERE?

...
I...

I WANTED TO THANK YOU.

YOU'RE SERIOUSLY OUT THIS LATE JUST FOR THAT?
NORMALLY IT'S NOT HARD FOR ME TO SAY WHAT I THINK.
BUT NOW...
I DON'T KNOW WHERE TO BEGIN.
MONICA, I THINK IT'S TOO LATE NOW.
I DON'T...
I DID IT ON PURPOSE.
THE RING.

I HAVEN'T WORN IT FOR A LONG TIME NOW.
IT'S HARD FOR ME TO SAY THIS,
BECAUSE OF MY FATHER AND MY KINGDOM...
BUT A WHILE AGO I DECIDED TO STOP FOOLING MYSELF.
...
MONICA, WHAT DO YOU...?

HEY...
MONICA...

NO!
!

IT'S TOO LATE FOR THAT, MONICA.

I NEVER KNOW HOW TO SAY THINGS.
AND DESPITE THAT, I CONFESSED MY FEELINGS TO YOU. TWICE.
YOU MADE IT CLEAR THAT WILLIAM, YOUR FIANCÉ, WAS YOUR PRIORITY.

I ONLY SAID THAT BECAUSE THAT'S WHAT I'VE BEEN TOLD MY ENTIRE LIFE!
THAT MARRYING WILLIAM IS MY DUTY!

THAT'S IT, THEN!

THERE'S NOTHING ELSE TO SAY.
I CAN'T THINK ABOUT THIS ANYMORE...
TOO MANY BAD THINGS HAVE HAPPENED...
WE SHOULD JUST FORGET ABOUT THIS.
FULFILL YOUR DUTIES AND MARRY HIM.
NO...
I'LL TRY TO FULFILL MINE AS BEST I CAN.
IT SEEMS LIKE YOUR FATHER MIGHT MAKE THINGS RIGHT, AFTER ALL...

IF MY MOTHER SEES REASON.

DORIAN...
I DON'T WANT YOU TO THINK I'M ANGRY WITH YOU.

I'VE KNOWN FOR A LONG TIME THAT WHAT HAPPENED BETWEEN YOU AND ME WAS SILLY...
I JUST DIDN'T THINK THAT YOU...

WELL, I'M SURE YOU'LL BE VERY HAPPY MARRYING WILLIAM.
SERIOUSLY.

THIS SOUNDS LIKE A FAREWELL.
NO!
I'LL BE LIVING WITH YOU AT THE PALACE, REMEMBER?

YOUR FATHER WILL GIVE US SHELTER UNTIL THIS SITUATION COMES TO AN END.

I TRULY BELIEVE THINGS MUST GET BETTER FROM NOW ON.

WAIT, SPIRIT!

IS IT HERE...?

ARE YOU SURE DORIAN'S HERE?

CHAPTER 51

WHOA!
DANI!!
WHAT A NIGHTMARE!
MARK, DUDE, WAKE UP!
POW
UGH...
IT'S AN EMERGENCY!
LEAVE ME ALONE, NICO. I WAS DREAMING ABOUT CUPCAKES...
I JUST DREAMED ABOUT DANI CRYING!
SHE WAS WEARING THE SAME WHITE DRESS AS IN THE VISION FROM THE CRYSTAL BALL.
CALM DOWN. SHE MUST BE ASLEEP BY NOW.
NOTHING BAD WILL HAPPEN TONIGHT. WE'RE SAFE HERE.
I HAVE A BAD FEELING.
I'M GONNA SEE IF SHE'S OKAY!
ZZZZZ...

SPIRIT...
ARE YOU SURE DORIAN'S HERE?

I CAN'T SEE ANYTHING...

IT'S SO QUIET...

WHAT'S THAT...?
IS THERE SOMEONE ON THE BED?
THEY'RE TOO BIG, THOUGH, THAT'S NOT DORIAN.

IT'S TOO DARK...
DON'T WORRY, YOUR EYES WILL ADAPT TO DARKNESS VERY SOON...

HUH...?
WHAT THE—?!

AH!
WHO'S THERE?
THERE ARE THINGS CHILDREN SHOULDN'T SEE.
MOM! WHAT ARE YOU DOING HERE?!
WHAT WAS THAT?
I THINK I SAW BLOOD... MOM...
DON'T WORRY, EVERYTHING IS OKAY. MOM IS HERE...
YOU'RE ALL GROWN UP!
YOU'RE SO PRETTY. YOU LOOK LIKE YOUR FATHER.
MOM, DAD IS—!
TSK!
WELL, IT DOESN'T MATTER NOW. LET'S GO FIND YOUR BROTHER.

DORIAN, OF COURSE, NOT DAMIEN.
DAMIEN DOESN'T SEEM TO AGREE WITH HIS FAMILY.
WE'LL MAKE HIM CHANGE HIS MIND.
ANYWAY, DORIAN IS THE KING WE WERE LOOKING FOR.
THEY'RE ALL SO IMPATIENT TO CROWN HIM.
NO!
WE WON'T GO ANYWHERE WITH YOU, MOM!
I DON'T WANT TO HURT YOU.
I JUST WANT YOU TO SPEAK TO THE KING, PLEASE.
TO FIX THINGS...
OH, SWEETHEART...
I'M SO SORRY, BUT THIS CANNOT BE FIXED.

WHERE DID THOSE TWO GO?!
HM...
WHAT'S THAT NOISE?
I HOPE IT HAS NOTHING TO DO WITH...
...THE TWINS.
WHAT A PAIR OF TROUBLEMAKERS.
AH...!

YOU'VE LEARNED SOME FUN TRICKS, DAUGHTER. HOW CUTE!
AND SUCH STRONG MAGIC, YOU CAN TELL YOU'RE A WYTTE.
BUT IT'S NOT ENOUGH. I'M PUTTING YOU TO SLEEP...
SO THAT YOU'LL COME WITH YOUR MOTHER.
GET AWAY FROM HER, WITCH!

DANI, ARE YOU OKAY?!
Y-YES, THANK YOU SO MUCH, NICO.
BE CAREFUL, THOUGH. SHE'S MY MOTHER!
THAT'S TRUE, I'M SORRY!
I GOT CARRIED AWAY. I SHOULD BE MORE CAREFUL WITH OLD PEOPLE.
THIS KID...?
WHAT A NUISANCE.
DIE!
NO!

WHERE IS HE?
DID HE ESCAPE...?
NICO—!
HUH?!
HE'S NOT HERE?!
HE'S GONE.
I SENT HIM AWAY WITH A SPELL.
AWAY FROM YOU.
DANI, GET OUT OF THERE.
A CHILD OF YOUR AGE SHOULDN'T SEE SO MANY BOD—

MOM... YOU...
YOU JUST TRIED TO KILL MY FRIEND.
WHAT'S WRONG WITH YOU?!
THIS IS RIDICULOUS... I CAN'T FORGIVE YOU, MOM.
I WON'T GO ANYWHERE WITH YOU!
SWEETHEART... YOUR FRIEND?
THESE PEOPLE AREN'T OUR FRIENDS.
THEY PRETEND TO CARE ABOUT YOU.
BUT AS SOON AS YOU DO SOMETHING TOO STRANGE FOR THEM WITH YOUR MAGIC, THEY'LL PUSH YOU AWAY.
OR WORSE.
I KNOW SOME PEOPLE ARE LIKE THAT, MOM, BUT NOT MY FRIENDS.
I'M VERY SCARY. WAY MORE THAN YOU, MOM...
INDEED! MINI NICO STRIKES AGAIN. HOW DO I ALWAYS END UP LIKE THIS?
BUT THEY ARE ALWAYS BY MY SIDE NO MATTER WHAT.
DANI, YOU DON'T GET IT—
OVER HERE!
I HEARD SOUNDS OF A STRUGGLE AND EXPLOSIONS!

HURRY UP!
IT'S CLOSE TO KING GEORGE'S CHAMBERS!
INTRUDERS, INTRUDERS IN THE PALACE!
LOOK, THEY'RE WITCHES!
THE GIRL IS ONE OF THE PEOPLE WHO SUPPOSEDLY SAVED US FROM THE DRAGON.
SHE BETRAYED US!
UH-OH...
NO!
CATCH THEM!
SPIRIT! HURRY UP, DO SOMETHING!
WHO ARE YOU ASKING FOR HELP, DEAR?
YOU CAN'T TRUST THESE PEOPLE.

NOBODY CAN HELP YOU.

BUT DON'T WORRY...
YOUR MOTHER WILL GET YOU OUT OF HERE, SWEETHEART.
STAY AND FIGHT, YOU COWARDS!
WE MUST PROTECT THE PALACE!
MAN, I'M NOT GOING TO FIGHT A DRAGON!

ARGH, DANI! WAKE UP!!
RUN!
IT BURNS!
THEY'RE FLYING AWAY!
STOP!
COME WITH ME, DEAR.
YOU'RE FINALLY WITH MOM...

AND SOON, WE'LL ALL BE TOGETHER.
DANI?
DORIAN,
DAMIEN,
YOU, AND I.
OUR FAMILY.
AGAINST THE REST.
LET'S GO, DARLING.
NOBODY WILL TRY TO HURT US.
AND IF THEY DO...
THEY WILL HURT.

CHAPTER 52

HOW COULD THIS HAPPEN?

WE DON'T KNOW, YOUR MAJESTY...

WE DON'T KNOW HOW SHE SNUCK INTO THE PALACE.

SHE'S A WITCH, AFTER ALL.

I'M NOT GOING ANYWHERE!

YOU MUST, DORIAN.

THEY MIGHT COME BACK FOR YOU.

YOU'LL GO WITH WILLIAM AND MONICA.

THIS PLACE ISN'T SAFE.

IS THERE SUCH A THING AS A SAFE PLACE?

WE COULD GO BACK TO THE HOUSE ON THE LAKE...

THEY TOOK DANI!!

I WON'T GO HIDE WHILE MY SISTER IS STILL OUT THERE!!

DORIAN—
I'LL RESCUE HER NO MATTER WHAT!

DORIAN, NO.
THAT'S WHAT MOTHER WANTS.
IF YOU GO BY YOURSELF, YOU'LL MAKE IT A LOT EASIER FOR HER.
MOM WON'T HURT DANI.

SHUT YOUR MOUTH!!
YOU DON'T CARE ABOUT DANI!!
I DIDN'T SEE YOU SHED A SINGLE TEAR OVER DAD!
THAT'S NOT TRUE.
BE HONEST, YOU DON'T CARE ABOUT ANY OF THIS!!
I DON'T TRUST YOU!!
HEY, LET HIM GO, DORIAN!

OH, HERE WE GO. YOU...!

...
HEH.

DON'T YOU SEE? HAVE YOU EVER DONE ANYTHING TO HELP?

I'LL GO LOOK FOR DANI,

NO MATTER WHAT YOU SAY.

NO.

...MARK? YOU, TOO? WHY—?

I'LL GO RESCUE DANI.
AND NICO.

HE'S IN GREAT DANGER, THEY DON'T CARE ABOUT KEEPING HIM ALIVE.

BUT, MARK... YOU HAVEN'T GOT MAGIC...
DORIAN, YOU'RE REALLY STRONG,
BUT YOU CAN'T BEAT YOUR MOTHER, YOUR AUNT, AND ALL OF THEIR FOLLOWERS BY YOURSELF.
YOUR MAGIC IS NO GUARANTEE.
BUT YOUR FACE AND SURNAME DRAW ATTENTION WHEREVER YOU GO.

I CAN GO UNNOTICED. THEY DON'T KNOW ME.

I'LL GO TO MONICA'S CASTLE.
THAT'S WHERE THEY'RE BASED.
I'LL WEAR A COSTUME AND GO UNDERCOVER.
AND I WILL GET THOSE TWO OUT OF THERE.
I'LL GO WITH YOU.
NO, AISHA!
I WON'T JUST SIT HERE AND DO NOTHING IN THE MIDDLE OF THIS WAR.
I'M ALREADY INVOLVED.
IF ANYTHING HAPPENS, AMIR WILL BE HERE TO PROTECT THE CITY.
YES, I...! I'LL DO ANYTHING I CAN!
I'LL STAY HERE WITH YOU, AMIR.
HOW ABOUT YOU, ANNE?
HUH?

BE CAREFUL!

SAME FOR YOU, IVY!

WE'LL SEE EACH OTHER AGAIN.

MARK...

BUT...
I NEED TO COME WITH YOU.

NO.
YOU MUST STAY WITH HER FOR NOW.

YOU NEED EACH OTHER, DORIAN.

AND DON'T GET ME WRONG, THIS ISN'T ABOUT ROMANCE.

...!

PLEASE, JUST...
TRUST ME.

HERE.
I WANT YOU TO TAKE CARLO WITH YOU.

WHAT...?!
BUT CARLO IS BASICALLY YOUR SON!
I KNOW YOU SAID MY MAGIC ISN'T A GUARANTEE,
BUT TAKING A LITTLE BIT OF MY MAGIC WITH YOU DOESN'T SEEM LIKE A BAD IDEA.

CARLO IS TINY. HE FITS IN YOUR POCKET AND HIS FIRE IS VERY POWERFUL, JUST LIKE A BIG DRAGON.
TREAT HIM WELL.
CARLO, BE CAREFUL!
I LOVE YOU LOTS!

I PROMISE I'LL BRING DANI BACK.

I'M COMING WITH YOU.
WHO'S THIS DUDE?
MASTER!?
I THOUGHT I'D GO UNNOTICED THIS WAY.

ALL RIGHT... NOW WE'RE READY!
WE'LL FLY TOTALLY UNDER THE RADAR. RIGHT...?
JEEZ, DUDE. YOU'RE CLEARLY NOT A NATURAL-BORN LEADER.
I AGREE... YOU SHOULD LEAD US INSTEAD, PRINCESS.

NOBODY'S LEADING NYONE! WE'RE A TEAM, NO POWER DYNAMICS INVOLVED.
SURE. OF COURSE.
OKAY, THEN. LET'S GO SAVE DANI AND BRING HER BACK SAFE AND SOUND!
WE'LL HAVE A CIVILIZED CONVERSATION WITH HER MOTHER!
AND WE'LL MAKE ALL THE WITCHES SEE REASON!
CAN'T WE ALL JUST GET ALONG?
OF COURSE, A CONVERSATION...
YES, INDEED, WE CAN ALL GET ALONG. ABSOLUTELY!

WHAT ABOUT THE BODIES...?
MONICA, DON'T THINK ABOUT THAT NOW.

BUT, WILL—!
DON'T WORRY. MY FATHER WILL BRING THEM TO THE CASTLE. THEN WE'LL BURY THEM.

I WONDER IF MOM AND DANI WILL ARRANGE DAD'S FUNERAL.

DON'T WORRY, YOUNG LADY.

I'LL TAKE CARE OF THE BODIES.
REST ASSURED.

FATHER!
KING EDGAR.

SO IT'S TRUE, THEN...
I NEED TO KEEP THESE...

...THINGS...IN MY CASTLE.
FATHER!

DON'T TALK LIKE THAT!
YOU DON'T GIVE ME ORDERS, WILLIAM.
LAST I CHECKED, I'M STILL YOUR KING.
AND THESE VERMIN AREN'T YOUR FRIENDS.
YOU SHOULD KNOW BETTER. BUT YOU'VE ALWAYS BEEN A BIT THICK, SON.

MONICA'S FATHER OFFERED HIM PROTECTION. YOU OWE IT TO HIM.
DON'T TALK TO YOUR FATHER LIKE THAT, WILLIAM.
THEY'RE WITCHES.
MOTHER—!

THEY'RE THE REASON KING GEORGE IS DEAD IN THE FIRST PLACE. HE TRUSTED THE WITCHES. WHAT A FOOL.

I FORBID YOU TO SAY THOSE THINGS ABOUT MY FATHER!
AND DON'T YOU DARE TOUCH MY FRIENDS!!
PRINCESS...
OR SHOULD I SAY MONICA?
YOUR FATHER'S KINGDOM IS IN MY CONTROL, AFTER ALL.
DON'T TRY TO BLACKMAIL ME LIKE THAT.
I'D RATHER BE A BEGGAR THAN LET YOU HURT MY FRIENDS. I WON'T GO WITH YOU IF YOU THREATEN THEM.
ME NEITHER.
WILLIAM, BEHAVE!
...

KEEPING THEM ALIVE WILL ONLY GIVE US FURTHER TROUBLE...
BUT THAT'S OKAY.
I WON'T BURN THEM...

AS LONG AS THEY BEHAVE.

I WANT TO COMFORT YOU.

AND I WANT YOU TO COMFORT ME.
I WANT TO TALK TO YOU, BUT I DON'T KNOW WHERE TO BEGIN.

I DON'T KNOW WHAT YOU'RE THINKING.
ARE YOU MAD AT ME?

DO YOU STILL THINK ABOUT ME?

IF YOU DON'T, I WON'T BLAME YOU.

I WANT TO HOLD YOUR HAND,

BUT THAT'S SOMEONE ELSE'S JOB NOW.

DORIAN.
!
YOU MUST GO LOOK FOR DANI.
...
YES.
I KNOW.
I WILL.
THANKS.

I'M SO GRATEFUL TO ALL OF YOU. THANK YOU FOR HELPING ME.

WITHOUT YOU...

SOLDIERS...
YOUR MAJESTY...
I DON'T KNOW WHERE I'D BE RIGHT NOW.
I'D L-LIKE TO PROPOSE A TOAST IN HONOR OF MY FATHER AND MOTHER...

THE KING AND QUEEN, SINCE AS YOU KNOW, THEY...
THEY...

MAY HE REST IN PEACE!
UGH...
OH, MONICA...!
TO THE KING.

TO THE KING AND QUEEN!
AND ANOTHER TO THE QUEEN!
DUDE, YOU'RE SUPPOSED TO BE DRIVING US TOMORROW!

DON'T YOU DARE, WILLIAM!
AGH!!
WHY NOT?! IT'S IN HONOR OF MONICA'S PARENTS! AND YOU'RE DRINKING TOO!

I'LL ALWAYS REMEMBER WHAT YOU DID FOR ME.

EVEN IF I DON'T EVER SEE YOU AGAIN.

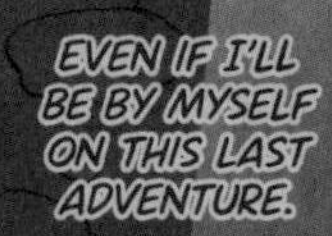

I'LL REMEMBER HOW STRONG AND BRAVE YOU WERE, THROUGH THE DARKEST TIMES.

THAT'S WHY I LOVE YOU.
HUUHH?!
WHAT ARE YOU DOING HERE?!
I'M COMING TO RESCUE DANI WITH YOU, OF COURSE!
YOU CAN'T COME! YOU JUST SUFFERED A TERRIBLE LOSS, IT'S NOT...
YOU DID TOO!
THAT'S PRECISELY WHY!
DANI'S THE ONLY PERSON I CAN STILL CONSIDER FAMILY! I NEED TO BRING HER BACK!

WELL, I DON'T HAVE A FAMILY!
BUT I CAN'T JUST CURL UP IN A BALL AND CRY WHILE MY FRIENDS ARE IN DANGER!
DANI AND NICO NEED US!

I'M NOT RUNNING AWAY WITH YOU, DORIAN!
I JUST WANT MY FRIENDS TO BE SAFE AND SOUND.

YOU'RE SAFER HERE.
YOU NEED TO GO WITH WILLIAM.
I'LL GO WITH WILLIAM. IT'S MY DUTY TO MARRY HIM.
DON'T WORRY, I DIDN'T FORGET THAT.

...ALL RIGHT, THEN.

LET'S GO.
STOP RIGHT THERE!
YOUR MAJESTY, THE MAGIC KID IS KIDNAPPING THE PRINCESS!
STOP THEM!!

UH...
UGH...
MY HEAD...

WHERE...?
WHERE AM I?
THIS ISN'T AMIR'S CASTLE...
AH!
NOW I REMEMBER!
MOM CAST A SPELL ON ME!
I NEED TO GET BACK TO DORIAN AND THE OTHERS!!

THEY MUST BE WORRIED SI— HUH?
IT'S LOCKED!
THEY LOCKED ME UP!!
UGH... THERE'S NO WAY... THE DOOR WON'T OPEN ONE BIT!
WHAT ABOUT MY WAND?!

OH...THEY TOOK IT, OF COURSE.
I'M TRAPPED.
WHAT AM I GONNA D—?

AH!! NICO!!
HE WAS WITH ME!
WHERE—?
I'M HERE!!
AHH!
WHAT ARE YOU DOING?!
I'M HIDING. CAN'T YOU SEE?
YOUR SPELL SUCCESSFULLY TURNED ME INTO A TADPOLE, ONCE AGAIN.
YEAH...BUT I DON'T THINK I CAN BRING YOU BACK TO YOUR NORMAL SIZE...
AT LEAST NOT UNTIL YOU'RE SAFE, SINCE I SHRANK YOU TO PROTECT YOU.
I KNOW, I KNOW. I'M STARTING TO GET A GRIP ON ALL THIS.
...
HEY... DANI...
DO YOU HAVE ANY IDEA WHERE WE ARE, NICO?
I'D RECOGNIZE THIS PLACE WITH MY EYES SHUT.
I'VE BEEN SLEEPING IN A MINIATURE VERSION OF IT FOR MONTHS.
HUH...?

YOU HAVEN'T REALIZED YET?
WE'RE IN MONICA'S ROOM.
WOW...
IT'S WAY GLOOMIER THAN I THOUGHT.
I DON'T THINK IT WAS ALWAYS LIKE THIS.
SO THEN MOM BROUGHT US TO THE CASTLE—?
MISS WYTTE...?
WHOA!!
POW
YOUR MAJESTY, YOU'RE FINALLY AWAKE!
WHO ARE YOU?!
LET ME OUT, I'M NOT A PRISONER!!
OF COURSE YOU AREN'T, YOUR MAJESTY!

WE'RE GOING OUT RIGHT NOW, AS SOON AS YOU'RE DRESSED TO ATTEND YOUR FATHER'S FUNERAL.
HUH?

RIGHT... DAD...
MISS, DON'T CRY.
I KNOW THIS IS A HARD SITUATION FOR YOU RIGHT NOW...

BUT THIS EVENT OPENED OUR EYES AND MADE US REALIZE WHO THE REAL KING OF WITCHES IS.
WHAT DO YOU MEAN?

IT'S CLEAR, ISN'T IT?
WE MADE A MISTAKE WHEN WE HANDED THE CROWN TO DAMIEN...
HE ENDED UP BEING A TRAITOR.

MANY WITCHES WOULD LIKE TO SEE HIS HEAD ON A STAKE, BUT THE MAJORITY ARE WILLING TO FORGIVE HIM.
WE CANNOT BUILD A SOCIETY UPON THE KILLING OF OTHER WITCHES.
BUT IN THE END, IT WILL BE UP TO THE NEW KING...

THE ONE WHO COMMANDED A DRAGON AND USED IT TO REMOVE HIS FATHER FROM THE EQUATION, SECURING HIS THRONE...

WE NEED A KING LIKE THAT, MAJESTY, A STRONG AND POWERFUL KING...

LIKE YOUR BROTHER DORIAN.

HOW DID THEY CATCH UP SO FAST?

IT'S OKAY, THEY CAN'T KEEP IT UP...

LET ME GO!
I NEED TO SAVE MY SISTER!
I HAVE HIS WAND, YOUR MAJESTY.
HE WASN'T KIDNAPPING ME!
I WARNED YOU...
AND I CARRY OUT MY THREATS.
YOU'LL DIE AT THE STAKE, YOUNG MAN.
NO!!
YOU BROUGHT THIS ON YOURSELF.

I NEED TO GET OUT OF HERE...
I HOPE YOU'LL BE ABLE TO REST TONIGHT!
WE'LL REACH THE CITY TOMORROW AND THEN...
WE'LL EAT ROASTED WITCH!
YUCK! THAT SOUNDS DISGUSTING.
SLAM
AND IN THE OTHER VAN...
WHY HAVE YOU TAKEN US PRISONER?
I'M THE PRINCESS! YOU CAN'T DO THIS TO ME!

SLAM
DAMIEN! DO YOU THINK THEY'RE GOING TO BURN US ALL?
NO...THEY JUST WANT TO KEEP AN EYE ON US.

THEY KNOW WE'LL TRY TO HELP DORIAN.
...AND I CAN'T ALLOW THAT, WILLIAM.
THE BOY BETRAYED US, AND HIS BROTHER AND PRINCESS MONICA WILL TRY TO PREVENT HIS DEATH.
YOU CAN'T DO THIS, FATHER!
DON'T WORRY, I WON'T HURT YOUR BELOVED "PRINCESS."
WE STILL NEED YOUR WEDDING TO SHIELD US FROM QUESTIONS OF OUR CLAIM TO THE THRONE.

ONCE WE GET RID OF THE WYTTE BOY, WE'LL CELEBRATE YOUR MARRIAGE.
YOU CAN'T BELIEVE THAT I'LL JUST SIT HERE AND WATCH.

ARE YOU SURE YOU WANT TO CHALLENGE ME, SON?
GO AHEAD, I HAVE QUITE A FEW SPARE CELLS.
UGH...

DID YOU HEAR?
YES...WHAT A TYRANT.
IT SEEMS LIKE THEY'RE GONNA BURN THE KID.
THE KID?!
PEOPLE SAY THE KID IS A WITCH...
BUT EVEN SO, I THOUGHT BURNING WITCHES WAS FORBIDDEN.
IT'S SUCH A CRUEL THING TO DO...
WHO CARES?
IT'S ABOUT TIME THEY TOOK CARE OF THE WITCHES, BEFORE THEY END US ALL.

...AND PRINCESS MONICA WAS CRYING AND SCREAMING!
WHO KNOWS WHAT THAT WRETCHED WITCH DID TO HER... HE'LL GET WHAT HE DESERVES.
REALLY? THOSE WITCHES ARE SCARY.

WELL, IT SEEMS LIKE OUR KING DORIAN IS IN SERIOUS DANGER.
I WONDER IF THE REST OF THE WYTTE FAMILY KNOWS.

THE WORST PART IS THAT THE NONMAGICAL PEOPLE ARE HAPPY ABOUT IT. THEY'RE SADISTIC!

WELL, THE WYTTES ARE THE ONES WHO KILLED THE KING AND QUEEN.
WERE THEY EXPECTING TO BE PRAISED FOR IT?
BE QUIET, SWEETIE!
DON'T SAY THOSE THINGS SO LOUD, YOU'LL BE SENTENCED FOR TREASON...
...
WHAT A BUNCH OF SNITCHES.
I DON'T KNOW WHO'S GOOD OR EVIL ANYMORE!
BUT I DO KNOW CHILDREN SHOULDN'T PAY FOR WHAT ADULTS DO. IT'S NOT THEIR FAULT.
DID YOU SEE HOW EASY THAT WAS? WE WENT COMPLETELY UNNOTICED.
YEAH, RIGHT... YOU'RE TOO RELAXED FOR MY TASTE.
AND YOU'RE WAY TOO TENSE.
YOU LOOK SUSPICIOUS WITH THAT THING ON YOUR FACE.
MARK...

I DON'T KNOW IF WE'LL GO UNNOTICED MUCH LONGER...
THAT POSTER IS UNMISTAKABLE.
WANTED
WAN

OH, CRAP.
COME ON, WEAR THIS!

TH-THANKS. BUT WHAT ABOUT YOU?
DON'T WORRY.
PEOPLE EXPECT PRINCESS AISHA TO BE A FORMAL GIRL WITH BRAIDS, ALWAYS IN PRINCE AMIR'S SHADOW.
YOU HAD BRAIDS?!
THEY DON'T SUIT YOU AT ALL.
AND WHY IS THAT??
IS THAT TRUE?
THEY'RE JUST RUMORS, BUT—
WE SHOULD GO TO THE CASTLE AND REPORT THIS...
YES, MRS. WYTTE NEEDS TO KNOW HER SON IS IN DANGER AS SOON AS POSSIBLE.
HUH?

I JUST HEARD THEY'RE GOING TO BURN DORIAN! WE NEED TO HURRY AND HELP HIM!
WE COULD CATCH A TRAIN, OR—!

WE COULD FLY!
MASTER, DO YOU THINK YOU CAN MAKE CARLO BIGGER?

WE CAN'T LEAVE NOW, WE'RE SO CLOSE TO DANI AND NICO—

DANI AND NICO AREN'T IN MORTAL DANGER, AS FAR AS WE KNOW.
HURRY UP.

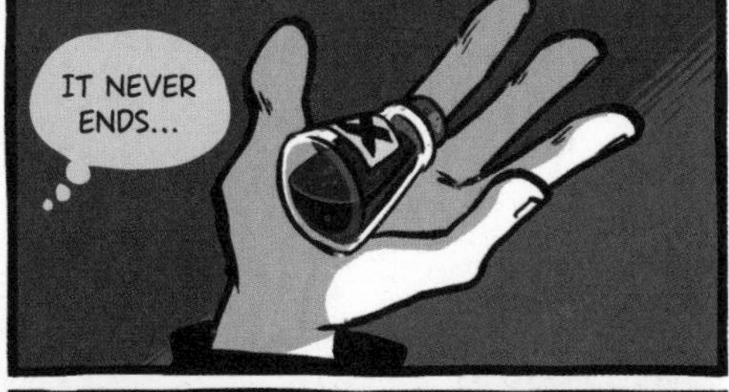
IT NEVER ENDS...

PERHAPS IT'S NOT TOO LATE TO CUT THIS PROBLEM OFF AT THE ROOT.

POOR THING... SHE MUST BE DEVASTATED ABOUT HER FATHER...
EVEN THOUGH IT WAS HER BROTHER WHO DID IT.
I WON'T HEAR A WORD AGAINST OUR FUTURE KING, DORIAN!
HE DID WHAT HE DID FOR OUR SAKES.

TRUE, TRUE. I CAN'T WAIT TO SEE THE BLACK CROWN ON HIM!
SOON HE'LL BE HERE, I'M SURE OF IT.

DO YOU THINK HE'LL COME RIDING HIS DRAGON?

MRS. WYTTE...

THERE'S SOMETHING YOU NEED TO KNOW.
THIS ISN'T THE TIME. HAVE YOU LOST YOUR MIND?
WE'RE SORRY, BUT THIS IS URGENT.
IT'S ABOUT YOUR SON, THE FUTURE KING, DORIAN.

HE'S IN DANGER.

CHAPTER 55

KNOCK KNOCK

WHO'S THERE?

IT'S ME, WILLIAM!

I'VE BEEN THINKING ABOUT IT OVER AND OVER...

HOW CAN I GET DORIAN OUT OF THERE WITHOUT GETTING ANYONE IN TROUBLE?

I DON'T MIND BEING IN TROUBLE, DAMIEN.

A BOOK...?

YES...
IT'S A BOOK OF DARK MAGIC...
BUT IT'S THE ONLY WAY TO SAVE MY BROTHER. I'LL DO IT FOR DORIAN.

WE'LL REPLACE HIM WITH SOMEONE ELSE WITHOUT ANYONE NOTICING.

REMEMBER, THE EXECUTION IS AT EIGHT. BEFORE THE SUN SETS. THE FIRST WITCH BURNING OF THE NEW ERA!
BOOKSTOR
I NEED TO HURRY UP AND FIND THAT BOOK!
COME ON, WILLIAM, FOCUS!
ONCE I FIND IT EVERYTHING WILL BE ALL RIGHT.
DAMIEN HAS A PLAN, LUCKILY...

TO REPLACE DORIAN WITH SOMEONE ELSE...
SACRIFICING A COMPLETE STRANGER, PROBABLY AN INNOCENT.
...
HE WOULDN'T DO THAT, RIGHT?

·Magic
·Music
erature &
rary studies
AH!
BINGO!

ONCE AGAIN, PRINCE WILLIAM'S SAVING THE DAY!
WHERE'D YOU LEAVE CARLO?
OUTSIDE THE CITY!
WE'LL GET DORIAN OUT OF THERE!
BUT YOU MADE HIM SMALLER, RIGHT?
OF COURSE!

BUT YOU CAN STILL TELL HE'S A MAGICAL CREATURE, AND WE NEED TO LIE LOW.
YES, WE NEED TO GO UNNOTICED!
I'M A GENIUS—!

ARGH!
UGH!
WILLIAM?!
AISHA!!
YOU'RE JUST IN TIME TO SEE HOW I'VE SAVED DORIAN!
DO YOU HAVE THE SPELL, DAMIEN?
AND NOW WHAT...?
...
PAY ATTENTION.
BY 6 PM, I URGENTLY NEED YOU TO BRING ME:

A FEW YARDS OF ROPE,
PURIFIED WATER,
THE URINE OF A PREGNANT LIZARD,
3 EUCALYPTUS LEAVES,
250 GRAMS OF SUGAR,
THE SEEDS OF THE VISION FLOWER,
A BIG, SHARP NEEDLE,
NOCTURNAL MUSHROOMS—
HANG ON, HANG ON, CAN YOU REPEAT THE COCKROACH PEE THING?
LIZARD URINE, WILLIAM!
PLEASE, WRITE IT DOWN...

WE DID IT... IT'S 6:15...
HOW'S THE SPELL GOING?
THAT WAS HARD.

EVERYTHING LOOKS GOOD. THERE'S ONLY ONE MORE THING I NEED...

AN UNFORTUNATE KID BETWEEN 11 AND 15 YEARS OLD WITHOUT FAMILY OR FRIENDS
SO THAT HIS DISAPPEARANCE WON'T ALARM ANYONE?

...
NO.

I NEED YOU TO FIGURE OUT HOW TO GET DORIAN OUT OF HIS CELL SO THAT WE CAN REPLACE HIM.
HURRY UP!
OKAY!

WAIT...
IF HE DOESN'T NEED ANYONE TO REPLACE DORIAN, IT MUST BE BECAUSE HE...
NO...!
DAMIEN!!
DON'T SACRIFICE YOURSELF BY TAKING DORIAN'S PLACE!
THERE MUST BE ANOTHER WAY!
WHAT'S THE MATTER?
DON'T DO IT!
WHAT ARE YOU TALKING ABOUT?
CALM DOWN, I WON'T SACRIFICE MYSELF.

ONLY THIS GUY HERE.
WHY DO YOU THINK I'VE BEEN SEWING ALL DAY?

WILLIAM?

GOOD!
THIS'LL DO!
AND...

...DONE?
IT DOESN'T EVEN LOOK LIKE A BROOM.

BUT I NEED TO DO SOMETHING!

I HAVE NO CHOICE.

LET'S GO!!

CHAPTER 56

WE'RE FINALLY HERE... I HOPE IT'S NOT TOO LATE...
THE STORM, THE HURRICANE WINDS, THE MIST...THIS TRIP WAS LIKE A BAD JOKE.

I KNOW THIS IS YOUR DOING...
YOU'LL BE SORRY IF WE GET THERE AND...IF DORIAN IS...

DANI, WHAT ARE YOU TALKING ABOUT?! PLEASE, LOOK AT ME!

I WASN'T TALKING TO YOU, NICO.
THEN WHO WERE YOU TALKING TO? DANI...?

EVERYONE'S READY.
THERE ARE MORE AND MORE PEOPLE IN THE SQUARE...
...AND I'M STUCK ON THE ROOF!!
WHAT A DISASTER!!
COME ON, JUST A LITTLE BIT OF BICEPS...
YOU CAN DO IT, MONICA...
UUUGH...
ARGH!
NO, I CAN'T.
LOOK, THE WITCH KID IS HERE!
DORIAN!!
OH, HE'S SO YOUNG THOUGH...
APPARENTLY HE WANTED TO KIDNAP PRINCESS MONICA...

I NEED TO GET OFF RIGHT NOW!

REALLY?! LET THEM BURN HIM!

DORIAN, HANG ON!!
UGH, FINALLY!!

THE KING NEEDS ME, RIGHT?

WILL'S FATHER WANTS US TO GET MARRIED, TO SECURE THE KINGDOM!

I'LL THREATEN TO THROW MYSELF OFF THE ROOF IF THEY DON'T STOP!

I'M SURE IT'LL WORK!!

I DON'T HAVE TIME TO GET DOWN, BUT I CAN...

SCREAM!
LISTEN UP, EVERYBODY!
STOP RIGHT NOW OR I'LL—!
MPH!
OH NO.
I DREW TOO MUCH ATTENTION.
WHAT CAN I DO?

SHHH, BE CAREFUL,
DON'T MAKE ANY NOISE, MONICA...
!
DORIAN!!
IS THAT REALLY YOU?!
YES, IT'S ME!
WH...?
WHAT THE...?!
HOW...?!
WHO'S THE GUY DOWN THERE, THEN?!
WELL... I DIDN'T REALLY UNDERSTAND IT...
BUT I THINK DAMIEN DID IT.

SUDDENLY MY CAPTORS WERE ON THE FLOOR, KNOCKED OUT.
MARK WAS DISGUISED AS A GUARD.
MASTER PENDRAGON WAS THERE, AND WILLIAM...
AND PRINCESS AISHA, WHO TOLD ME WHAT I HAD TO DO.
IT WAS A SMALL SACRIFICE...
COMPARED TO THE IMPRESSIVE RESULT.

THAT PUPPET IS MY SPITTING IMAGE.
UH...
I'LL HAVE TO THANK DAMIEN WHEN I SEE HIM AGAIN.
INDEED!
BUT RIGHT NOW WE JUST NEED TO GET OUT AS QUICKLY AS POSSIBLE!
WHAT?
NO!
WAIT!
NO, NO, NO, MONICA!
YOU MUST STAY!
WHAT...?
JUST FOR ONCE, STAY OUT OF THIS.
DAMIEN'S PLAN WILL ONLY WORK IF THE KING BELIEVES I'M DEAD.
YOU CAN'T COME WITH ME, OR THEY'LL THINK I KIDNAPPED YOU AGAIN.
YOU'RE SAFE HERE.
THE KING IS A TERRIBLE MAN, BUT HE WON'T HURT YOU.

I NEED TO FIND DANI AND NICO.
I NEED TO SAVE MY SISTER FROM MY MOTHER'S GRASP.
SHE'S ALREADY SPENT TOO MUCH TIME THERE.
I'M SO WORRIED ABOUT HER.
I'LL BE BACK SOON!
DON'T DO ANYTHING FOOLISH. I KNOW WHAT YOU'RE LIKE, MONICA!
HUH?!

FINE!
I'LL BE VERY QUIET THIS TIME, BUT I KNOW THAT I COULD HELP!
I ALREADY KNOW THAT ALL TOO WELL!
I WISH YOU ALL THE BEST!!

I WAS SHAKING WITH HELPLESSNESS.

I COULDN'T STAND WATCHING DORIAN FLY AWAY ON HIS BROOM,
WHILE I WAS JUST STANDING THERE DOING NOTHING.

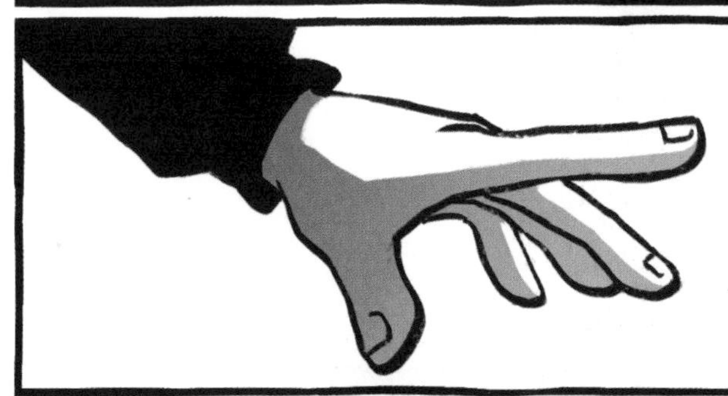
BUT I KNEW THAT FOR ONCE, MY MOST HEROIC DEED WAS LETTING HIM GO.

WHAT?

FORGET WHAT I SAID THE OTHER DAY.
PLEASE, DON'T MARRY HIM.
I'LL BE BACK SOON, I PROMISE.
WHA...?
OKAY.

WAIT FOR ME UNTIL THEN.

BUT...WHEN ARE YOU COMING BACK? HOW SOON?

THE CRIES OF THE PEOPLE AND THE SMELL OF SMOKE FILLED THE AIR.

THAT WAS THE LAST TIME I SAW DORIAN.

IT HURTS...
IT HURTS SO BAD,
THERE ISN'T ROOM FOR ANYTHING ELSE.
UGH...
UH...
DORIAN...
...
SNIFF...
THIS CAN'T BE.
MAKE IT STOP.
IT DOESN'T MAKE SENSE.

NOTHING DOES.
HOW DID WE GET TO THIS POINT?
WH...?
UGH...
HOW COULD I ALLOW THIS TO HAPPEN TO THEM?
AH...
ALEX...

DAD...
DANI...
DANI, I...
AND I CAN'T GO BACK.
UH...
IT'S TOO LATE.

I COULDN'T SAVE YOU.
DORIAN...
DORIAN, I'M SORRY...

I DIDN'T MEAN TO...

I LOVE YOU SO MUCH...

I CAN'T HELP IT, DORIAN. I ATTRACT NEGATIVE STUFF...

IT DOESN'T MATTER NOW...

THERE'S NOTHING LEFT...
UGH...
IT HURTS TOO MUCH...
IT'S TOO MUCH...
MAKE IT STOP.
DANI?

I'M SO SORRY, I—
IT'S OKAY, NICO.
IT'S OKAY.

•EXTRAS•

CHAPTER 40⅔
I'M BORED!
I'M SICK OF WATCHING YOU GET BEATEN UP, WILLIAM.
THIS SUMMER WE ARE YOUR GUESTS, ENTERTAIN US.
I'VE GOT IT!
WE COULD PLAY HIDE-AND-SEEK AROUND THE PALACE.
GOOD IDEA!
DAMIEN, DO YOU WANT TO PLAY TOO?
WHO'S DAMIEN?
MY FRIEND AND BUTLER!
...
THAT CREEPY GUY'S BEEN WATCHING US ALL THE TIME?

DO YOU WANT TO PLAY HIDE-AND-SEEK, DAMIEN?
HUH? I...
I DON'T PLAY!

OF COURSE YOU DO!
ONE...
TWO...
THREE...

NINETEEN...

AND TWENTY!
I'M COMING TO GET YOU!

OKAY, I'M WELL HIDDEN HERE...
I JUST HAVE TO CONCENTRATE ON NOT TRANSFORMING ANYONE INTO AN ANIMAL...
DON'T
RANSFORM
DON'T
TRANSFORM
DON'T
TRANSFOR
DON'T

HEY, DAMIEN!
CAN I HIDE IN HERE WITH YOU?!
AAAARGH!

UH...
UGH...
WILLIAM...
OH NO, WILLIAM!
I'M SO SORRY!
IT'S JUST...
YOU SCARED ME!
I'M...
BUSTED!

OH, I...
I THOUGHT WILLIAM WAS HERE WITH YOU.
HA-HA, NO, HE'S NOT!
NOT AT ALL.
WELL, YOU LOST.
YOU'RE ALL GONNA LOSE, I'M COMING FOR YOU.
STEP STEP STEP
PHEW...
THAT WAS A CLOSE ONE.
ALTHOUGH STILL...
I CAN'T CLAIM VICTORY.
WILLIAM...
I HOPE SOMEDAY YOU CAN FORGIVE ME...
BEING YOUR FRIEND HAS BEEN THE BEST THING THAT EVER HAPPENED TO ME.

THANK YOU FOR EVERYTHING, WILLIAM.
THAT WAS AMAZING!
WHAT?
THANKS TO YOUR MAGIC I DIDN'T LOSE THE GAME!
DAMIEN, YOU'RE GREAT!
ARE YOU SERIOUS?
OF COURSE!
IMAGINE THE POSSIBILITIES!
SOME TIME LATER...
POP QUIZ, YOUR HIGHNESS.
HOORAY, POP QUIZ!
DAMIEN, PLEASE!
I HAVEN'T STUDIED AT ALL!
THAT'S THE FIFTH TIME YOU'VE ASKED ME THIS WEEK.
I'M NOT GOING TO TURN YOU INTO A RAT ANYMORE.
THE END

CHAPTER 40⅔
IVY, PASS THE BUTTER PLEASE.
IT'S RIGHT THERE ON THE TABLE.
PRINCESS...
OH, HELLO DAMIEN!
WHAT ARE YOU DOING?
WE'RE MAKING CHOCOLATES FOR LOVERS' DAY.
YES, AND PLEASE LET'S FINISH THIS BECAUSE IT'S A DRAG.
I'M ONLY DOING IT BECAUSE AMIR INSISTED THAT HE WANTED MY CHOCOLATES.
REALLY?
HE ASKED ME TOO.
WHAT?
THAT BRAT'S GOING TO FIND OUT!
AND YOU, PRINCESS,
I GUESS YOU ARE MAKING CHOCOLATES FOR PRINCE WILLIAM?
NOPE.

THEY'RE TO GIVE TO THE NEW STABLE BOY.
MY TRUE LOVE!
OH NO.
POOR WILLIAM.
LOOK, HOW MUCH THEY LOVE ME, HAHAHA.
NOT LIKE YOU.
NOBODY LOVES YOU!
NOOOOO!
BAH, SO WHAT.
IT'S NOT LIKE HE'S GOING TO BE TRAUMATIZED BY THIS.
I CAN'T DO ANYTHING ANYWAY.
RIGHT?

THE GIRLS ARE BAKING SWEETS FOR US!
LET'S GO PEEK!

LET'S SEE...
WOW! LOOK HOW CONCENTRATED THEY ARE!
IT SMELLS SO GOOD!
MY STOMACH'S RUMBLING ALREADY!
AH!

DAMIEN!?
LOOK AT HIM, COOKING WITH ALL HIS LOVE!
HOW SWEET...
I WONDER WHO HE'S MAKING CHOCOLATES FOR...
WHAT A MYSTERY!
DON'T TELL ME THAT...
YOU'RE A CHEAT, DAMIEN!
YOU'VE INFILTRATED TO EAT ALL OUR CHOCOLATES!
WHAT ARE YOU TALKING ABOUT, YOU FOOL?!
WILLIAM, AS SHARP AS ALWAYS.
THE END